D1577232

SAJO
AND HER BEAVER PEOPLE

SAJO
AND HER BEAVER PEOPLE

GREY OWL

BISHOPSGATE PRESS LTD

Edited by Sheila Elkin

Jacket illustration by David Arthur
Jacket design by Gill Harris

Originally published 1935 as
THE ADVENTURES OF SAJO AND HER BEAVER PEOPLE

This edition © Bishopsgate Press Ltd. 1988

British Library Cataloguing in Publication Data

Grey, Owl
Sajo & her beaver people
I. Title
823'.912 [J]

ISBN 1-85219-035-3

All enquiries and requests relevant to this title should be sent to the publisher, Bishopsgate Press Ltd., 37 Union Street, London SE1 1SE

Printed by Biddles Ltd., Guildford, Surrey.

CONTENTS

1. Beaver house.
2. Interior of beaver house. The living-room, or chamber.
3. Sleeping platform.
4. Lower level for drying off, draining into plunge-hole.
5. Plunge hole.
6. Tunnel leading out into deep water.
7. Side, or emergency entrance, also used in discarding old bedding and used sticks.
8. Main entrance.
9. The dam.
10. Spillway, for regulating overflow, and maintaining correct water level.
11. Trees felled, and partly felled by beaver.
12. Bottom of pond.
13. Feed raft. Greatest portion under water, below the reach of ice.
14. Beaver runway, or hauling trail, used for removing required portions of tree, cut down by beaver.
15. Original stream resuming its course.
16. Stream running into pond.
17. Bottom of pond has been dug out below the feed raft and in front of the dam, so as to obtain a greater depth of water. The materials thus obtained are used in the construction of the dam and house.
18. Former dry land, now under water on account of dam. Without the dam there would be no pond, only the stream.

CHAPTER ONE

GITCHIE MEEGWON, THE BIG FEATHER

Early one morning, a lone Indian in a birch-bark canoe paddled up the broad, swift current of the Yellow Birch river. He was tall, with keen dark eyes, and his long black hair fell in two braids over his shoulders. He was dressed in a suit of fringed buckskin that had been smoked to a rich brown and wore moccasins on his feet. For this was in the days before the white man had reached this great lonely land of forest, lake and river beyond the settlements of Northern Canada with their roads and railways. And the Indian, whose name was Gitchie Meegwon – the Big Feather – looked much like the Indians you see in old films.

His canoe was bright yellow, dyed with the juice of alders, and the seams along its sides were sealed with narrow strips of shiny black spruce-gum, to keep the water out. This canoe had a large eye, like that of some enormous bird, painted on the front of it, and behind, at the very end, was fastened the tail of a fox, which swayed gently back and forth in the breeze. For the Indian liked to feel that his canoe was actually alive, and had a head and a tail like all the other creatures, and was sharp-eyed like a bird, and swift and light like a fox. In it there was a neatly folded tent, a small bag of provisions, an axe, a tea-pail, and a long, old fashioned rifle.

From the tops of the birches on the hillsides there came a low whispering, a sound of rustling that never seemed to cease, as the wind played among the leaves, so that the Indians had named these highlands the Hills of the Whispering Leaves. The river banks were lined by a forest of tall, dark pine trees, and their huge limbs hung out over the water, far above it; along the shore beneath them robins, blackbirds and canaries flew and fluttered, searching for their breakfast among the new grasses and the budding leaves of the pussy-willows. The air was heavy with the sweet smell of sage and wild roses, and here and there a humming-bird shot like a brilliant purple arrow from one blossom to another. For this was in May, called by the Indians the Month of Flowers.

Gitchie Meegwon belonged to the Ojibway nation; he had paddled against the strong current of the Yellow Birch river for many days, and was now far from his village. Steadily, day after day, he had forged ahead, sometimes moving along easily on smooth water, at other times poling up rough rapids, forcing his frail canoe up the rushing, foaming water and between jagged, dangerous rocks with a skill that few white men and not all Indians learn. This morning his way was barred by a waterfall, higher than the tallest pine trees, where the sun made a rainbow in the dashing white spray at the foot of it. Here he landed, just beyond the reach of the angry, hungry-looking whirlpool that tried very hard to pull his canoe in under the thundering falls. Picking up the canoe, he carried it, upside down on his shoulders, over a dim trail between the giant whispering trees, a trail hundreds of years old, and on which the sun never shone, so shaded was it. He made a second trip with his possessions, loaded his canoe, and then continued his journey in the brightness and the calm water above the falls.

He glanced sharply about, as the bends in the river opened up before him, and saw many things that would have escaped the eyes of anyone but a hunter: an exciting glimpse of a pair of furry ears pointed his way, the rest of the creature hidden, or of bright eyes that gleamed out at him from the shadows; and once he saw a silver-coated lynx fade like a grey ghost into the underbrush. Here and there deer leaped hastily away towards the woods, whistling loudly through their nostrils as they bounded like red rocking-horses through the forest, their tails flashing like white, swaying banners between the trees. Once he came upon a great moose, as big as any horse, who stood chest deep in the river, his head buried under the surface while he dug for lily roots on the bottom. As Big Feather paused to look at the moose, who, busy with his task, had not heard him, the huge creature raised his head and stood there staring in surprise, while the water poured in streams from his face and neck. Then he turned and plunged ashore and soon was gone, though the heavy thudding of his hoofs and the sharp crack of breaking limbs and small trees could still be heard for a minute or two as he galloped crashing through the woods.

Even with all this company, Gitchie Meegwon was a little lonely, for back at the village he had left his two children, a girl and a boy. Their mother had died, and though the women of the village were kind to them, they missed their mother very much, and he knew they must be lonely too, as he was. The three of them were great friends and were seldom parted, and usually their father took them with him. But this time he was alone, as this was likely to be a dangerous journey, for he expected to have trouble with some poachers before it was finished.

Gitchie Meegwon had built a fine log cabin for his small family, for a summer home, and there they had been happy and comfortable together, resting after the hard winter's hunt, when word had been brought in by a friendly Cree Indian that a band of half-breeds from down near the settled country had invaded the region, and were killing all the beaver. The real bush Indians do not hunt on each other's trapping-grounds, considering such behaviour to be stealing, but these town-bred half-breeds had given up or forgotten the old ways, and were liable to clean out every trapping-ground as they came to it. And without fur with which to buy provisions at the trading post, Big Feather's family would go hungry. So here he was, deep into his winter hunting-ground, to protect it from these strangers. But he had seen none of them nor any sign of them, and the weather being now warm, and fur-animals no longer worth stealing, he felt that his work was done. Tomorrow he intended to turn back for home.

With these pleasant thoughts in mind, he was passing along close to the river bank, watching for any tracks which the careless half-breeds might have left, when all at once he smelt a strong, sharp scent upon the air – some beast, or perhaps a man, had passed near by and crushed the spicy-smelling leaves of a mint plant. Instantly on the alert, he glanced quickly at the bank, when suddenly a short, dark, heavily-built animal sprang out into the river right in front of his canoe and sank like a stone, out of sight. Almost immediately a black head and a brown, furry back came floating up a short distance away, and the creature swam rapidly round the canoe until, cleverly getting to a spot where the wind was from the Indian to himself, he caught the man-scent, that all the Forest People fear so much. Down came his wide, flat tail on the water with a terrific splash, the water flying in all directions as he dived like a flash, this time for good.

Big Feather shook a few drops from the sleeve of his leather shirt, and smiled; this was very much what he had wanted to see. It had been a beaver. And before the echo of the beaver's alarm signal had died away, there came another from around the next bend, sharp and loud, almost like a gunshot. There were two of them.

The Indian smiled again, for now he began to feel sure that no one had hunted here. These Beaver People would have been only too easy to catch; if these careless fellows, who allowed him to get so close to them, right on a main highway so to speak, had not been captured, the rest of them must all be safe. Still, to make certain, he decided to visit their home, where there should be others. Their

10

house would not be hard to find, as beaver, when on their travels, cut small green saplings of alder, poplar and willow here and there, eating the bark off them, and these peeled sticks show white and shiny every place they land, so one has only to follow from one to another of these feeding-places to discover where they live. Very soon the Indian came to where a little stream ran down into the river, and at its mouth he found what he expected – a number of these slim, shining sticks, remains of a beaver's meal. No doubt their house would be somewhere up the little stream, in some quiet spot such as beaver love.

The beavers had eaten at the edge of a nice open point where a few giant pine trees stood about, as though they had wandered out from the forest and could not get back again. Here Gitchie Meegwon made a small fire and had his own noon meal. Indians drink a good deal of tea on their travels, so, leaning a slim pole over the cheerful blaze, he hung his tea-pail on one end of it to boil, the other end being stuck firmly into the ground to hold it in position; he arranged strips of deer-meat on sharp forked sticks before the hot coals, and under them placed slices of Indian bread, or bannock as it is called, to catch the delicious gravy that fell from the meat as it cooked. After he had eaten he smoked quietly for a little time, listening to the humming of the breeze in the wide, fan-shaped boughs of the pines. Very like music it sounded to him, and he leaned back contentedly and watched the patterns made by the lazy smoke.

Soon, after covering his goods with the overturned canoe, he took his long-barrelled gun and started up beside the brook, on his way to the beaver pond that he knew must be at the head of it. His moccasins made no sound, and left no track, as he walked softly in the quietness and calm of the sleepy forest, while squirrels shrilled and chattered at him from the boughs, and whisky-jacks, those knowing, cheerful camp birds to be

11

seen nearly everywhere in the woods, followed him from tree to tree, sometimes getting ahead of him to peer wisely and whistle at him as he passed. He enjoyed the company these small creatures gave to him, and took his time and walked quite leisurely along, when suddenly he stopped, listening. His keen ears had caught a strange, unexpected sound, which quickly became louder and louder and was all at once a roar – and then he saw, coming swiftly down the creek-bed towards him, a rush of yellow, muddy water, bringing with it a mass of sticks and litter which filled the banks to the very top and went pouring by in a wild, swirling torrent. Something terrible was happening up at the beaver pond! It could be only one thing: some man or beast, something, must have torn out the beaver dam, and this rushing torrent was the beaver's so carefully-saved-up water, without which they would be helpless.

In a moment, rifle in hand, Big Feather was leaping and tearing his way through the forest that had but a moment before seemed so pleasant, and was now so dark and threatening. Forward he raced at top speed to save the beaver colony from destruction, springing high over logs, smashing his way through windfalls and branches and tangled underbrush, bounding like a deer through the shadowy woods towards the pond, hoping he would be in time. Well did he know what had happened!

Negik, the otter, bitter and deadly enemy of all the Beaver People, was on the war-path, and the beaver, their water gone, must even now be fighting for their lives.

CHAPTER TWO

THE HOME OF THE BEAVER PEOPLE

Before the otter broke the dam, the scene at the beavers' home had been very different. Walking beside the bustling creek, you would have come quite suddenly upon a small, deep pond. Right across the front of this pond, and blocking the stream that came out of it, was a thick, high wall of sticks and brushwood. It was all very tightly woven, and the chinks were filled with moss and the whole business well cemented with mud. Along the top of it a number of heavy stones had been placed to keep it solid. It was nearly thirty metres long and more than a metre high, and the water flowed over the top of it through a narrow trough of sticks, so that the stream was wearing away at it in only this one spot, where it could be easily controlled. So well had it been made that it looked exactly as if a gang of men had been working at it – but it was animals, not men, that had built it.

This wall, which was really a dam, seemed as if it were holding the lake in place: which is what it was doing, for without it there would have been no lake at all, only the stream running through.

The pond was bright with sunshine; very silent and peaceful it was, back there among the Hills of the Whispering Leaves, and so calm, that the few ducks dozing quietly upon its waters seemed almost to be floating on air, and the slim white poplar trees that stood upon its banks were reflected so plainly on its smooth surface, that it was hard to tell where the water stopped and the trees began. It was very beautiful. And it was very still, for nothing moved there, and it seemed quite lifeless except for the sleeping ducks. Yet, had you watched

13

patiently for a little while, being careful not to move or talk, or even whisper, you would have seen, before very long, a ripple on the water near the shore as a dark brown head, with round ears that showed very plainly, peered cautiously out from the rushes at the water's edge, and watched and listened and sniffed. The head was followed by a furry body, as its owner now came out in full sight and swam rapidly, but without a sound, to another place on the far shore, there to disappear among the reeds. The tall reeds swayed and shook for a minute as he worked there, and then he reappeared, this time holding before him a large bundle of grass, and swam over towards an enormous black mound of earth that rose from the surface of the water, and dived, bundle and all, right in front of it. He had scarcely disappeared before another head, with another bundle, could be seen swimming from a different direction when – somebody moved, and with no warning at all, a huge flat tail came down on the water with a heavy smack, and with a mighty splash and a plunge the head and its bundle were gone. Now, this was exactly what had happened to Big Feather, down on the river that morning, and for the same reason. For that great mound, taller than any of us, before which the swimmers had dived, was a beaver house, and the dark brown, furry heads were those of the beaver family. And they had been very busy.

The lodge had been built up to more than two metres in height, and was a good three metres across. It had lately been well plastered with wet mud, and heavy pieces of wood had been laid on the slopes of it to hold everything firmly in place. It looked very strong and safe, like a fortress, and even a moose could have walked around on top of it without doing it a bit of harm. Up the side of it there was a wide pathway, on which the building materials were carried, and had you been patient and careful, and lucky enough not to have the wind make your presence known to those keen noses, you might have seen old father beaver dig out a load of earth from the shore. You would have seen him swim slowly and carefully with it to the mound and then, standing upright like a man, walk to the top of the roof with the load in his arms. There he would dump it, pushing it into nooks and crannies with his hands, and shoving a good-sized stick in after to keep it there.

All this work had been done with a purpose. It was a very important time, this Month of Flowers, for inside that queer-looking home, hidden away from the eyes of all the world, were four tiny little kitten beavers. Woolly little fellows they were, perfectly formed, with bright black eyes, big webbed hind feet, little hand-like fore-paws and tiny, flat, rubbery-looking tails. They had marvellous appetites, and their lungs must have been very good too, for they were the noisiest little creatures imaginable, and cried continuously in long, loud wails that were very much like the cries of small human babies: and like any other babies, they needed a great deal of attention – and you may be sure that they were getting a lot of it too.

The living-room inside the lodge, was large enough for a man to have curled up in with ease, and was very clean and sweet smelling, with its floor of willow bark and bed of scented grasses. The entrance was through a short, slanting tunnel, one end of which, called the plunge-hole, was in the floor, and the other end came out below, near the bottom of the lake. The dam held the pond up to a level nearly even with the floor, keeping the plunge-hole always full, so that the tiny kittens, who were a little wobbly on their legs as yet, could drink there without falling into it; or if they did (which happened rather regularly), they could climb out again quite easily. The whole tunnel and the outer doorway were under water, so that no land animals could enter, or even see it, unless they were first-class divers, which most of them are not. But if the dam should break and let the saved-up water out, the beaver would be in grave danger, as not only could their enemies, such as wolves and foxes, find their way into the house, but the beaver would be unable to protect or hide themselves by diving suddenly out of sight.

If you look at the sketch you can see how it was all arranged, and will be able to realize how very important this dam was, and why the father spent so much of his time watching it and fixing any small leaks that appeared. He had, too, a pretty steady job keeping the trough, which you might call a regulator, clear of rubbish, so that the water could flow freely and not become too high, and so flood the house, but was always at exactly the right level. Between whiles, both he and the mother attended to their babies' every want, changing their bedding every so often, bringing in small sprays of tender leaves for them to eat, combing and brushing their wool (you could hardly call it fur), while they made queer, soft sounds of affection and talked to them in that strange beaver language that, at a little distance, sounds almost as though human people were speaking together in low voices. And the shrill wailing cries of the little ones, and their chattering, and their little squawks and squeals, could be heard even through the thick walls of the lodge, so noisy were they when they were hungry, or pleased or in some small trouble, which, one way and another, was pretty nearly all the time. And when either their father or their mother returned (they were never away together; one or the other was always on guard) from a trip to the so-important dam, or brought in new bedding of sweet-grass, he or she would give a low, crooning sound of greeting, to be immediately answered by a very bedlam of loud shouts of welcome from the youngsters, that went on long after it was at all necessary. They were never still unless they were asleep, and were continually scrambling around, and tussling together, and clambering over everything, and by the noise they made, seemed to be enjoying themselves immensely. And altogether they were pretty much like any other family, and were very snug and happy in their home.

The little ones were now old enough to try their hand at swimming in the plunge-hole, though at present this exercise consisted mostly in lying on top of the water, not always right side up, and going round and round in circles, screeching with excitement. And being so very light, and their fluffy coats containing so much air, they could not seem to sink deep enough for their webbed hind feet to get a grip on the water both at the same time, so they swam with first one foot and then the other, rolling from side to side and bobbing up and down, squirming and squealing and wriggling, while their parents passed anxiously around among them, giving them encouragement, or perhaps advice, in their deep, strong voices.

But the kittens would soon become tired and, climbing out on to the drying-off place (a little lower than the rest of the floor, so the water would soak away and not run all over the beds), every little beaver carefully squeezed, rubbed and scrubbed the water from his coat on the front, sides, back, every place he could reach, sitting upright and working very industriously, puffing and blowing like most of us do after a swim. Then, when this was all over and everybody was dry, or thought he was (some of them would topple over once in a while and made rather a poor job of it), the call for lunch would go up in a loud chorus, and the new green leaflets and water-plants that had been provided ahead of time (with the idea, no doubt, of putting a stop to the uproar as soon as possible), would be divided up, and pretty soon all the busy little jaws would be munching away, and the piercing cries died down to mumbles and little mutterings of contentment. And soon the little voices became quiet and the small black eyes closed, while they lay cuddled together on their sweet-smelling, grassy bed, with their tiny fore-paws, so much like hands, clutched tightly in each other's fur.

This would be their daily programme until, after perhaps three weeks, would come that glorious day when they would venture down the long, dim tunnel out into the brightness of the great unknown world that was all about them, but which they had never seen. And while they slept the old ones stood watch and guard, turn about, and took turns to inspect the defences of their castle and the dam on which their very lives depended, and kept a weather eye out for enemies, and collected food and bedding for when the babies should awaken, and carried on at the hundred and one jobs that make father and mother beaver a very busy pair of people during the latter part of May, the Month of Flowers.

The four kittens had just arrived at that thrilling stage when they could at last dive without bobbing up immediately, tail first, like a rubber ball, and could swim around on the surface for quite a respectable distance without calling loudly for help, when one day at noon, when Gitchie Meegwon was busy at his dinner, the father noticed that the water in the entrance was sinking. He watched it for a moment; the mother too heard it gurgling and came to look – the water was going down, swirling into the tunnel – was gone!

Someone had broken the dam!

Into the empty plunge-hole, one after another tumbled the two big beaver. There was no time to be lost. They were losing their precious water, the water upon which the lives of their little ones depended! Their home was open now to all the world; it might mean the death of all of them. The four kittens, terrified, realizing that something fearful was wrong, but too young to know just what it might be, crept close together, whimpering, while their alarmed parents tore through what was left of the water,

18

towards the dam.

They found a hole, nearly as big as a barrel, right at the deepest part of it, where it would quickly drain the lake to the very bottom. Madly the beaver began to work, pulling down sticks from anywhere, tearing out great armfuls of earth from the marshy shore, slashing off limbs from fallen trees with their razor-sharp teeth, rolling stones into the hole and shoving grass and brush in between them, digging up mud and pushing it before them into the break, where the suction of the now rapidly-falling water held it plastered tight against the sticks and stones and brush. But the pond had been too small for so big a leak, and water was not coming in from the tiny stream that fed it nearly as fast as it was going out.

And now that the dam was almost repaired, the pond was empty!

Despair seized on the beaver as they worked (don't let anyone ever tell you that animals cannot feel despair!), but they never gave up until the very last load was in its place, and then, their task at length finished, they turned and plodded wearily and unhappily back towards their four little babies in the house, useless now as a protection – the house they had worked so hard to build, the babies that they loved so very much. Beaver are slow walkers, and what had once been a short, easy swim had now become a slow, awkward scramble through slippery mud and over rocks and tangled, fallen water-plants and weeds. Precious minutes would pass before they would have staggered, and crawled, and dragged their way to that dark mound that now seemed so far away. Anything could catch them. If a bear or a wolf should pass and see them they would have no chance; the Beaver People were defenceless now, for they were never made to fight, only to work.

Hurry! Hurry! Gitchie Meegwon, run your fastest; your Little Brothers need you badly, need you now!

Across the muddy bottom of the empty pond the two big beavers struggled slowly, painfully and pitifully on their short and weary legs towards their unprotected home and babies, while – within the lodge, huddled together, their tiny hands clutched tightly in each other's woolly fur, four helpless little kitten beavers stared in terror at a sleek, black monster with a flat, evil head, that crept slowly through the entrance towards them, his teeth bared, hissing like a snake as he came. Negik the otter, the hungry, the cruel and the sly, having broken the dam and so drained the pond, could now get what he had come for – kitten beaver meat! Now was his time. His snaky body blocked the plunge-hole; there seemed to be no escape. He gathered his legs beneath him, ready to spring.

Just then Gitchie Meegwon, breathless, his shirt off, his gun ready, burst through the reeds beside the dam, and leaping from rock to rock, made for the beaver house.

CHAPTER THREE

THE FIRST ADVENTURE

The otter sprang. But in his eagerness, so greedy he was, he tried to seize them all at once, and the little beavers, quick as so many coiled springs, threw themselves sideways in the way that beaver have, and scattered before him as he came. Aiming at no particular one, he missed them all, nearly stunning himself against the wall of the lodge with the force of his leap. This confused him for a second, and the kittens rushed past him through the entrance, now no longer blocked by his body. The otter, roused to ferocious anger by his failure, and knowing very well that he could catch them one by one outside, was about to turn in pursuit, when the doorway was again darkened. That was all the warning he had. The next moment he was fighting for his life with the two big beavers. They had arrived only just in time; and they, usually so playful and good-natured, would fight to the death in defence of their young ones.

The otter was quicker on his feet and fiercer than they were, and could lock his jaws like a vice once he had bitten in, like a bull-dog; but a beaver's hide is tough, and their chisel-shaped teeth, that could hew down big trees and had never before been used to do harm to anyone, now slashed through skin and muscle, inches deep. They held on with their hands and drove their razor-edged cutting-teeth in deeper and deeper. The otter fought hard, for he was no coward, trying for his favourite hold on a beaver's nose and mouth, so as to prevent at least one of them from using his teeth. But he had all he could do to defend his own throat, at which the beavers were aiming. He twisted and turned like a great hairy lizard, lashing out right and

21

left with his snaky head, hissing, snapping, and snarling. The beaver held on in deadly silence, while he dragged them here and there, and they drove their teeth in again and again. For here was an enemy, the worst one of them all, who must be got rid of somehow – anyhow. Fighting fair with this evil beast was only a waste of time; the matter must be settled once and for all. Over and over they fought and wrestled and rolled, until they rolled right out through the plunge-hole, a squirming, tangled mixture of legs, tails and glistening teeth, almost at the feet of Gitchie Meegwon, whose last flying jump from one rock to another had brought him close beside the beaver house. The sight of this new foe discouraged the otter completely, and with a violent effort he broke loose and in one leap was beyond the beavers' reach. Paying no attention to the Indian, they scrambled after the fleeing otter, but the slimy mud that held them back gave the otter just the kind of going that he needed. He threw himself forward in the slippery ooze and slid, then took two or three jumps and another slide, and kept this up until he was at the dam, and over it, and away – for ever.

Never again would he make war on beavers.

Big Feather, standing on a near-by rock, saw him go. Once he aimed his rifle at the otter, but thinking he had punishment enough he let him go. Anyway, everything was all right now, and water was beginning to collect again. A good-sized pool had already formed in the basin of the pond, getting larger all the time, and held there by the dam, which the beavers had so swiftly repaired. Big Feather was obliged to hurry back to shore before the rocks became covered again. However, he was still a little anxious, as he had seen the young ones rush out, but had not seen them go back in. So he sat down on the shore, in a spot where he could be neither seen nor smelled, and watched the goings-on. Soon he saw the mother beaver return to collect her little ones. Two of them had come out of hiding, and as she came for them in turn, each would mount upon her broad, fat tail, which trailed behind her like a short toboggan, and standing upright on it and holding on to his mother's fur with his hands to steady himself, would be dragged across the mud to the doorway. And the little fellow would look around as he rode on this queer conveyance, taking in all the sights, no doubt feeling mighty pleased with himself. I think Big Feather got as much fun out of it as the kittens did; he saw two of them taken home this way, and laughed to himself at the comical sight. And as he watched, he could not help feeling, somehow, that it was a great shame ever to kill such creatures, that worked so hard to protect their babies and their humble home and seemed to have such real affection for each other – almost like killing little people, he thought. He had never before seen such things, and he began to realize why some of the older Indians called the beaver Little Talking Brothers, and Beaver People.

Although he had neither food nor blanket, he made up his mind to stay all night in case the otter should return, or another one come, for they often travel in pairs. But none did, and when Gitchie Meegwon left next morning he saw that the pond had filled up completely, and was running over as before; the secret doorway was again hidden, and everything was in good order, and the same as it had ever been.

That is, nearly everything. What he did not know was, that two of the kittens, scared almost out of their wits, had scrambled on and on until they found themselves near the dam. Trying to get as far away as they possibly could from that fierce monster, and hardly knowing or caring where they went, they had slipped over the dam unobserved. They had gone on down the now dry and empty stream-bed, hearing in their excited imagination the hissing breath of Negik close behind them. So real did this become to them, and so near did it seem to be at last, that

23

they scrambled hastily under a hollow in the bank – and not a moment too soon. For they were scarcely out of sight before the otter went hurrying by; they really *had* heard him. Fortunately, baby beavers, like the very young of many other animals, give out no scent, so that not even a fox, for all his sharp, inquisitive nose, could ever have found them except by accident. So Negik never knew they were there, and kept on putting as much ground between himself and the beaver pond as he could, after the beating he had got there.

Too terrified now to move lest their enemy should return, the two mites clung together in their shelter, afraid to go ahead, afraid to turn back. So they waited for their mother, who would be sure to look for them. But that lack of scent that had just now saved them from the otter, was to be their undoing. For their parents, searching frantically everywhere, could not trace them, and did not know they had even left the pond; and in their excitement and fear the kittens had not noticed how short a distance they had really come. So, like two tiny lost children, they sat miserable and lonely in their little cave, listening for a deep, crooning voice that they loved, waiting, waiting for the big kind mother who had always comforted them in their small troubles and kept them warm with her brown, furry body, and had combed and scrubbed them so carefully every day. Surely she, or their father, who had played so gently with them and taught them how to swim, and had always brought them sweet-grass for their beds and sprays of tender leaves for them to eat – surely he would soon come for them! But now there were no sweet-grasses, no juicy tender leaflets, only hard rocks and gritty sand; and no father, no mother came for them. And so they crouched together all the long night, shivering, hungry and afraid.

Once a slim, dark creature, the shape of a weasel but much larger, peered in at them, and they waited, still as two mice, scarcely daring to breathe, while he sniffed loudly at the opening where they were hidden, and then passed on. It had been a mink who, seeing two of them together, had feared to attack them. Later on they peered out cautiously from under the bank, but ducked back just in time to escape a great, grey shape that swooped down at them from above, an awful, ghostly creature with huge, staring yellow eyes, that missed them only by a wing's breadth and swooped up again, to sit on an overhanging branch, from where it stared and stared, and snapped its beak and gave loud, long screeches, and made a horrible chuckling sound.

Wap-aho, the Laughing Owl of the woods, had spotted them and was waiting patiently for his chance. And every time they peeked out from their hiding-place, the dreadful yellow eyes were there, staring down at them.

At daylight the owl was gone, and as the dam was full again and spilling over by now, the stream was running freely. And on its flow they now set out to find their home. If they had only known how close it was! But they were entirely lost and, too small to swim against the current, they went the easiest way and floated with it, slipping down, down the stream, further and further away from their parents and the home where they had romped and played so happily all their short lives.

On they floated, weak and hungry for want of the leaves and plants they did not know how to look for; yet they felt a little safer now that they were in the water once again – drifting along on this fruitless journey that could have only one ending. As the little stream began to reach the level of the Yellow Birch it flowed more slowly and became quieter and quieter, and they floated easily and smoothly upon its lazy waters. Once a deer, feeding in a shallows, looked up and saw them, watched them with his gentle eyes, his long ears pointed forward. Further on they met a hurrying muskrat, who gave them a sharp chitter of greeting and passed them by. Birds looked down on them and called to them from the tree-tops, far above; and the sun was warm and pleasant, and the world was very beautiful as they floated sleepily, dreamily along – to nowhere. And so they would go on, dreamy with hunger and weakness until, as sick little beavers do, they would fall asleep at last and never wake.

And then, as they floated out on to the broad, calm waters of the Yellow Birch, Gitchie Meegwon saw them.

He had been back at his dinner place again, at the foot of the stream, and quietly launching his canoe he paddled softly over to them. They heard him, opened their eyes a little and saw him. Somehow they were not afraid, as he lifted them into the canoe by their tiny black tails. Perhaps they didn't care any more, or maybe the big, watchful eye painted on the front of the canoe didn't look so sharp and fierce as it was intended to. Perhaps too, they knew he wouldn't harm them; for animals, even very young ones, seem to know who is their friend.

He handled them gently, for they were very small and pitiful as he held them cupped in the hollow of his two hands. Their wee front paws were tucked up in feeble little fists, as though to put up some kind of a little fight for their tiny lives; but the chubby heads were too heavy and drooped down, and their eyes were closed. Big Feather knew they must be dying, and was sorry for them, for he was a kindly man, as hunters so often are, when they stop to think.

He would try to save them. After all, he thought, he had made his living by killing beaver for their fur, and it seemed only fair that in return he should do something for these two lost waifs that had drifted almost into his hands. On shore, he took from his provisions a can of milk, and making a thin mixture of some of it with water, poured a little in their mouths. And as he held the small woolly bodies gently in his big brown hands, he could feel how

26

flat and empty their little stomachs were, and how feebly
the little hearts were beating. And as he fed them they
clutched tightly at his fingers with their tiny hands. And
his heart softened more and more towards them as he fed
them, though he hardly knew what he was going to do
with them. He had little time to spare, as he had promised
Sajo and Shapian, his children, that he would be back on a
certain day, and he did not want to disappoint them. If he
carried the kittens back to the pond they might never find
their way across, and if he let them go here they would
certainly starve, or else the hawks, or an eagle, or even a
hungry fish would get them. But he had far to go, and they
would be a nuisance; after all, they were only little animals
– yet, they were in great trouble and needed help, and he
felt that it would be wicked to abandon them; for some of
the old-time Indians had very strict rules about such
things.

Their mother had thought them beautiful; but the
Indian found them to be very unattractive indeed, with
their big hind feet, short, round little bodies and little pug
noses. In fact, they were so ugly that really they were
almost cute, he finally decided; just the thing for pets!
Sajo, his daughter, was nearly eleven years old, and was
soon to have a birthday. They would make a perfect
present – the very thing! And when they became too big to
have for pets, they could be brought back to their old
home again. Just then, feeling the effects of the milk, they
began to cry for more – those voices! They quite finished
Gitchie Meegwon – how could a man desert two creatures
that were able to cry so much like children? He thought of
his own children when they had been small, at the same
time pouring some more milk down the hungry little
throats.

And so he cut a large sheet of tough, leathery bark from
a fine birch tree that stood close by among the pines, and
with it made a strong, light box, or basket, with strips of

cedar wood to hold it in its shape, and made a close-fitting lid that fitted neatly down over the top of it, and punched it full of holes for air, and made a handle of braided cedar bark to carry it by. And inside it he put some bedding of grass and rushes, and green food-stuffs such as he knew that beaver loved. And when he lifted them in by their little flat tails (they made a first-class handle!), and they smelt the nice clean bed of sweet-grass, the very same as they had always had at home, and found the tender buds and leaves that they had wanted so badly; and what with the kind, soothing voice of their new friend, and with – oh, one thing and another, they suddenly felt very much better.

And they forgot the otter with his hissing, fishy breath, clean forgot the owl with his staring yellow eyes and fiercely snapping beak, who had laughed at them so grimly in the darkness. And they jabbered together with little bleats and squeals, as they had not done this long time past, and ate and ate until they could hold no more.

And Big Feather, as he dipped and swung his paddle in his swift canoe, on his way back to his home and loved ones, was very pleased with the gift that he would bring his children (of course the boy, who was three years older than his sister, would have to share in the fun too, even though it was not his birthday); and he was glad because he had helped two suffering forest creatures. And speaking to the canoe, or his gun, or maybe to the little beavers, or perhaps just talking to himself, he said:

"Mino-ta-kiyah, it is well! Kae-get mino-ta-kiyah, it is well indeed!"

And the two small adventurers must have found things to be going very well with them, too, as they had become very quiet. And indeed, they were very comfortable in their nest; and they could hear, through the air holes in their birch-bark basket, the song of the blackbirds and the thrushes, and the cheerful gurgling of the water all around; heard the drowsy humming of the insects and all the other pleasant woodsy sounds. Yet, even in this new-found happiness, they did not quite forget, never would quite forget, the kind father and mother, and the old home and small companions they had lost; and they were lonely for them all at once, and whimpered a little and crept together, and held each other tight. And then the loneliness would go away again, when they were close together; and so they fell asleep.

And that is how two small, lost, kitten beavers – so small that both of them could have sat together very comfortably in a pint-jug – went on their way to a new home and friends, and saw many strange and wonderful things that the wisest of beavers had never even heard about, and had adventures such as no beaver ever had before.

It was indeed, as Big Feather had said, mino-ta-kiyah – really quite first class, in fact!

CHAPTER FOUR

SAJO'S BIRTHDAY

One day, almost a week later, Sajo and Shapian were busy preparing for their father's homecoming. Gitchie Meegwon's home was a short distance away from the Indian village of O-pee-pee-soway, which means The Place of Talking Waters. The Indians had so named the village on account of a low waterfall that was near by, where the bubbling and the murmuring of the water made a sound like that of low, dreamy voices, so that the people said that there were spirits in the falls.

The cabin in which the children lived was built of pine logs, and stood not far from the lake shore, on a grassy knoll. The forest started right behind it, but the ground all around had been cleared of underbrush and fallen timber, leaving only the finest trees, which formed a glade through which there was a splendid view of the lake. This lake was a large one, and the farther shore showed only as a range of tumbled, forest-covered hills that seemed to be rolling for ever on into the blue distance, like the waves of some great, dark ocean. A narrow footpath, or water-trail, led down the slope from the cabin to the landing. There stood a grove of tall and graceful poplar trees, in whose leafy shade Gitchie Meegwon and his young son and daughter spent many a happy day beside the water.

The cabin was not large, but it looked handsome from the outside, with its walls of red-brown logs and rows of green and yellow moss between them. Though it had only one room, it was even more pleasant to look at on the inside. The floor, of solid logs hewed flat and fitted tight together, had been scrubbed until it was as clean and bright as any floor you ever saw, and on the three bunks

30

that stood in a row along one wall, rich-looking Hudson's Bay blankets were neatly folded. Some of them were red, some were white and others green, each with wide black stripes at either end, and they made the place look very bright and cheerful. The three windows, a single large pane of glass in each, were as spotless and shining as windows ought to be, as shiny as the inside of a rifle barrel, so Shapian put it; for that was his idea of something that was very clean indeed. That was the way he kept his own rifle, and today it had been oiled and rubbed, inside and out, till it fairly glittered in its corner, opposite the door where anyone who entered could not help but see it. For this rifle, which had cost him four good mink skins at the trading post, was the proudest of all his possessions, which, I may tell you, were not very many.

Sajo had gathered the stems of bulrushes and dried them, and then cut them into short lengths and dyed them blue, and red, and yellow, and threaded them, like long, narrow wooden beads, on strings, and these hung down in rows beside the windows. She had arranged the different colours to make a kind of pattern, and they had quite an expensive look about them – rather like curtains, she thought, as she glanced at them for about the hundredth time.

On the table, all the tin dishes and knives and forks had been arranged in their proper places, and in the centre was a large loaf of Indian bread, or bannock, as it is called, freshly baked and still steaming hot, and stuck upright in the top of it was a very small spruce tree no higher than your hand. It was really a tiny Christmas tree, and although it was not Christmas time, Sajo was nearly as happy as if it had been, and that was her way of showing how she felt about everything. The little iron stove that had been polished until it looked like a new one, had no oven and no legs, and was raised some distance from the floor on flat stones, which was a very convenient

31

arrangement, as, to bake bread, all you had to do was to cook the dough for a while on top of the stove, and then you put it underneath, between the warm stones, where it got finished off and nicely browned by the heat from the fire above.

Shapian had done his part too, as could be seen by the large pile of wood in a box behind the stove, and the rug of deerskin, newly stretched and dried, that lay in the centre of the floor; while in a huge pot upon the stove were cooking all the choicest portions of the meat – obtained with that so-much-prized rifle in the corner. Shapian was a manly-looking boy, tall for his age, with the copper-coloured skin and dark eyes of his people, the Ojibways. He sat quietly waiting; his father had set this day for his return, and when he promised something he always kept his word, as nearly as the uncertainties of forest life would allow. But his sister, younger than he, her brown eyes a-glow and her jet-black hair, in two long braids, flying behind her, ran and hopped and skipped from place to place, tending to the cooking, placing around the table the the rough wooden blocks they used for chairs, and putting the finishing touches to the wooden curtains.

Shapian had seated himself where he could get a good view out across the lake, through one of the windows, and was watching for the first sight of Big Feather's canoe – though he pretended not to be, and had chosen a window on the far side of the room, through which he could keep an eye without appearing to do so; as it would never do, he thought, to show how anxious he was. He was just fourteen, and he was feeling quite grown-up just now, as he had been the head of the household for well over a month. Sajo sang a little song as she worked, and was all a-flutter with a many-coloured tartan dress, and on her feet was a beautiful pair of beaded moccasins, worn only on special occasions. For this was to be a big day for her; not only was her so-loved father coming home, but it was her birthday. Poor Sajo! She did not often get a birthday gift since her mother had been laid to rest beneath the wild-flowers, but she still had two wooden dolls her father had made for her on two different birthdays. This year he had been away, and would have had no time to make her anything. So the two dolls, Chilawee and Chikanee by name, had been brought out and were sitting on the edge of one of the bunks, not looking particularly cheerful, though they too were all dressed up in tartan plaid, the same as Sajo was, and their complexions, which had either soaked in or run off, had been renewed with a paint brush, and they each had a little head-shawl round their wooden faces. They *did* look rather dumb, come to look at them; they had neither fingers nor noses nor mouths, but it is very likely that they didn't know the difference, and they would have to do for this time. As Sajo went so happily about her tasks, Shapian sat very still and watched across the room, through his window. He wished that his sister would be a little more dignified and not act so wild and excited – still, two such big events as these, coming both together on the same day, must be rather unsettling to a woman, he supposed. And then his own heart began to beat a good deal faster, and he had all he could do to keep from rushing to the window; for out on the lake far, far away, he saw a tiny speck.

"Sister," he said, speaking slowly and distinctly, as was his fashion, "our father is coming."

"Where! Where!" cried Sajo, and without waiting for an answer she snatched up her head-shawl and ran out through the door, looking eagerly in every direction. "Where, show me, quick!"

Shapian pointed out over the water, to the speck. "There," he said. "That little spot."

"Oh," said Sajo, and her voice fell a little; that spot could be anything. "Maybe it's a bear or a moose swimming," she suggested, hoping he would say it wasn't.

But an answer came before he had time to speak.

Far off, faintly, they heard a sound, a faint, sharp crack – a rifle shot; and then, right away, another. They listened; there was a pause while you could count three, and then another shot.

"The signal! The signal!" cried Sajo, and Shapian replied quietly, "Yes, it is our father's signal," and then, quite forgetting himself, turned and rushed into the cabin with her, saying: "Let us get ready quickly." And although the canoe was still some miles away and would not be in for at least an hour, there was a great bustle as they went to work. They ran to the shelves for the jars of preserved blueberries and wild strawberries that Sajo put by every year (these were really the first she had ever done all by herself, but she had made a good job of them), and they put on the big tea-pail to boil, and stuck a long iron fork into the meat to see if it was cooked, and ran from table to stove and from stove to table and back again, and altogether they acted a good deal like any other children would have done on such an occasion, whether they were rich or poor, or royalty, or just a couple of little Indians.

And when at last the yellow bark canoe, with its watchful eye and swaying tail, slid to a stop upon the sandy beach, everybody began to talk at once. Gitchie Meegwon stepped out on the shore and took their hands, or as many of them as he could hold, in one of his, while he held the other, for some reason, behind him, and tried to answer all the questions at once, while his face, that could look so stern, was full of smiles and laughter.

"Children, children, let me speak, give me a chance to speak – yes, I am safe; no, I didn't see any half-breeds; and yes, our hunting-ground is not disturbed – or no, I should have said, and yes, I was lonesome, but not now, and – happy birthday to you, my Sajo; happy birthday, my little daughter," and not till then did he bring out from behind his back the other hand. And in it was the birch-bark

34

basket, which he held by its braided handle beyond their reach.

"Gently, gently! See, I have brought you a gift for your birthday, Sajo," and gave it to her and told her to carry it with great care, while he turned to Shapian and added, "For you too, my son; there are two of them."

"Two of what, Father?" asked the boy, looking after his sister, who had started away. "What is in the basket?"

But Big Feather said he must wait and see. And they followed Sajo to the cabin as she went up the pathway at a funny little gliding run, supposed to be jolt-proof, so that while the small beaded moccasins twinkled in and out from under the tartan dress at a great rate, her body was held as stiff as possible from the knees up, so as not to jar the basket, which she held out in front of her as though it were a large and very delicate egg that would break into a thousand fragments at the slightest shock. Very carefully indeed she went, for out of this mysterious box there came the strangest sounds. A baby, she thought; no, two babies – though it seemed they must be very little ones to be in so small a space. Once inside, she set the basket very gently down upon the floor, and while Shapian (he had lost no time on the way either) held the sides, she took off the lid, and looking inside saw two small, round woolly bodies and four little paws that reached for the edge of the box like tiny hands, and two pairs of bright black eyes.

"Oooh!" she breathed, a kind of a gasp it was. "Oh! Oh!" And that's all she could say, and could think of nothing else to say and so cried "Oh!" again; and at last: "Teddy bears, live teddy bears!" (Teddy bears were all the rage at that time, and I think that every child in all the world either had a teddy bear, or wished for one). Then she turned the basket gently on its side and out they came; and she saw their tails, and knew then what they were! Better than teddy bears – .

"Little beavers, it's little beavers," burst out Shapian,

35

pale with excitement, his youthful dignity gone to the four winds. "Real ones, alive!" And Big Feather stood smiling down at the two delighted youngsters, very pleased indeed to see how well his present was received.

Sajo sat beside them in wonder on the floor, her mouth still an O, but no sound was coming out of it any more. She was too busy to draw her father's attention to the curtains she had been so proud of, and the dinner was kept waiting, and the famous gun, so clean and shiny, stood fogotten in its corner.

Gitchie Meegwon had looked after the kittens very carefully on the long journey, and had fed them well. Now they were round and fat, and cuddly-looking, and Sajo thought they were the cutest things she had ever seen. And when they clambered on to her knees with little shaky whimpers, she bent down over them, and rubbed her face on their soft wool, that smelled so sweet from their bed of scented grass and willow bark. Soon Big Feather and Shapian went out to find fresh leaves and bedding for their small guests; but Sajo stayed behind. And while these two were away, she picked up the little beavers and held their dumpy bodies, one at a time, in her two small hands, where they fitted very comfortably, and whispered softly to them – and, wonder of wonders, they answered her in little childish voices, and held on to her fingers with their wee hands (you could call them nothing else), and looked at her very attentively out of their bright black eyes that seemed somehow to look so very wise. And when she held them both together in her arms they made funny little sounds, and pushed their warm, damp noses tight against her neck, and blew and puffed, as little babies do.

And she knew that she was going to love them very much.

And in that plain log cabin, far back in the forests of the Northland, there were that day three very happy people:

36

Gitchie Meegwon, because his homecoming had been such a glad one; Shapian, because his father had given him too, a share in the beaver and had praised his work besides; and Sajo, because of the most wonderful birthday gift that she had ever had.

CHAPTER FIVE

BIG SMALL AND LITTLE SMALL

The kittens quickly took a liking to their new way of living, and although no human beings could ever quite take the place of their own parents, everything possible was done to make them feel at ease.

Shapian partitioned off the under part of his bunk with sheets of birch bark, leaving one end open; and this was their house, in which they at once made themselves very much at home. Gitchie Meegwon cut a hole in the floor and fitted down into it a wash-tub, for a pond – not much of a one, perhaps, but it was as large as the plunge-hole had been, and they spent nearly half their time in it, and would lie on top of the water eating their twigs and leaves. Whenever they left the tub, they always squatted their plump little persons upright beside it, and scrubbed their coats, first squeezing the hair in bunches with their little fists to get the water out. That done, the whole coat was carefully combed with a double claw that all beavers are provided with, one on each hind foot, for this purpose. All this took quite a while, and they were so business-like and serious about it that Sajo would become as interested as they were, and would sometimes help them, rubbing their fur this way and that with the tips of her fingers, and then they would scrub away so much the harder.

It was their fashion, when drying themselves off in this way, to raise one arm high up above their heads, as far as it would go, and rub that side with the other hand, and being upright as they were, it looked as if they were about to dance the Highland Fling. They often sat up while eating the bark off small sticks, and as one or other of them held a stick crossways in his hands, rolling it round and round while the busy teeth whittled off the bark, he looked for all the world like some little old man playing on a flute. Sometimes they varied the show, and when the stick was very slim they ate the whole thing, putting one end in their mouths and pushing it in with their hands, while the sharp front teeth, working very fast, chopped it into tiny pieces. The rattle of their cutting machinery sounded much the same as would a couple of sewing-machines running a little wild, and as they held up their heads and shoved the sticks, to all appearances, slowly down their throats, they looked a good deal like a pair of sword-swallowers who found a meal of swords very much to their taste.

They had to have milk for the first two weeks or so, and Sajo borrowed a bottle and a baby's nipple from a neighbour in the village and fed them with it turn about. But while one would be getting his meal (both hands squeezed tight around the neck of the bottle!), the other would scramble around and make a loud outcry and a hubbub, and try to get hold of the bottle, and there would be a squabbling and a great confusion, and the can of milk was sometimes upset and spilled; so that at last there had to be another bottle and nipple found, and Shapian fed one while Sajo fed the other. Later on they were fed bannock and milk, which made things a little easier, as each had his own small dish which the children held for him. The beavers would pick up the mixture with one hand, shoving it into their mouths at a great rate; and there was a good deal of rather loud smacking of lips and hard breathing to be heard, and they often talked with their mouths full. But they had one excellent habit, and liked to put away their dishes when they had finished, pushing them along the floor into a corner or under the stove. Of course if there was a certain amount of milk-soaked bannock left in them, that was quite all right, so far as the beavers were concerned, and by the time the dishes had arrived at their destinations these remains had been well squashed and trampled on the line of march, and the floor would be nicely marked up with small, sticky beaver tracks. Being fed separately, each of them came to look on one of the children as his special friend, and one of them would go to each when they were called. At first they had no names, and the children just called "Undaas, undaas, Amik, Amik," which means "Come here, come here, Beaver, Beaver." But a little later on Sajo remembered the day that the two wooden dolls had seemed to be looking on when the kittens first had come, and how these new arrivals had so quickly taken their place; well, she thought, they may as well take their names as well, and so she called the beavers Chilawee and Chikanee, which means Big Small and Little Small. And the larger one of the two was called Chilawee, or Big Small, and the not-so-large one was called Chikanee, or Little Small. And so they both got their names; which suited them very well too, because, after all, they *were* very small and they *did* look a lot like a pair of woolly toys that had come to life and stepped down from a shelf. And it was not long before they got to know these names, and would always come out from the house under Shapian's bunk when called; but the names sounded so much alike, that when one was called they both would come, and as they themselves were very much alike, the difference in size being not very great, it was often pretty hard to tell which was which. And to make matters worse, they did not grow evenly; that is, one would grow a little faster than the other for a while, and then he would slack down and the other would catch up, and get ahead of him. First one was bigger than the other, then the other was bigger than the one! And it would be discovered that Little Small had been Big Small for quite some time, while Big Small had been going around disguised as Little Small.

It was all very confusing, and Sajo had just about

40

decided to give them one name between them and call them just "The Smalls," when Chilawee settled matters after a manner all his own. He had a habit of falling asleep in the warm cave under the stove, between the stones, and one day there was a great smell of burning hair, and no one could imagine where it came from. The stove was opened and examined, and swept off, and the stove-pipes were tapped, and rapped, but the smell of burning hair was getting stronger all the time; until someone thought of looking *under* the stove, to discover Chilawee sleeping there unconcernedly. The hair on his back had scorched to a crisp, and he was routed out with a large patch of his coat badly singed. This made a very good brand, something like those that cattle are marked with on a ranch, and it made it very easy to tell who was who; and by calling one of them (the burnt one) *Chil*awee, and the other Chik*anee,* so as to be a little different, they each got to know their name, and everything was straightened out at last.

They were a great pair of talkers, Chilawee and Chikanee, and were always jabbering together, and sometimes made the strangest sounds. Whenever either of the children spoke to them, which was often, they nearly always answered in a chorus of little bleats and squeals. When there was any work going on, such as the carrying in of water, or wood, or the floor was being swept, or if the people laughed and talked more than usual, or there were any visitors, the two of them would come bouncing out to see what it was all about and try to join in, and they would cut all kinds of capers, and get pretty generally in the way. It had been found that if given any titbits from the table, they always took them into their house to eat or store them. So when they, like bad children, got to be something of a nuisance to the visitors, they had to be bribed with bits of bannock to make them go back in again; but before long, out they would come for some more bannock, and take that in with them, and out again, and so on. And very soon they got to know that visiting time was bannock time as well, and when meal-times came around they knew all about that too, and would be right there, pulling and tugging at the people's clothes and crying out for bannock, and trying to climb up people's legs to get it. And of course they always got what they wanted, and would run off with it to their cabin under the bunk, shaking their heads and hopping along in great style.

They followed the children around continuously, trotting patiently along behind them; and their legs were so very short and they ran so low to the floor on them, their feet could hardly be seen, so that they looked like two little clockwork animals out of a toy-shop, that went on wheels and had been wound up and never *would* stop. Anything they found on the floor, such as moccasins, kindling wood and so forth, they dragged from place to place, and later, when they got bigger and stronger, they even stole sticks of firewood from the woodbox and took them away to their home where they sliced them up into shavings with their keen-edged teeth and made their beds with them; and nice, clean-looking beds they were too. Any small articles of clothing that might happen to fall to the floor, if not picked up at once, quickly disappeared into the beaver house. The broom would be pulled down and hauled around, and this broom and the firewood seemed to be their favourite playthings; chiefly, I suspect, on account of the noise they could make with them, which they seemed very much to enjoy.

But their greatest amusement was wrestling. Standing up on their hind legs, they would put their short arms around each other as far as they would go, and with their heads on each others' shoulders, they would try to put each other down. Now, this was hard to do, as the wide tails and the big, webbed hind feet made a very solid support and they would strain, and push, and grunt, and blow until one of them, feeling himself slipping, would begin to go backwards in order to keep his balance, with the other coming along pushing all he could. Sometimes the loser would recover sufficiently to begin pushing the other way, and then the walk would go in the opposite direction; and so, back and forth, round and round, for minutes at a time, they would carry on this strange game of theirs, which looked as much like two people waltzing as it did anything else. All the while it was going on there would be, between the grunts and gasps, loud squeals and cries from whoever was getting pushed, and much stamping of feet and flopping of tails, trying to hold their owners up, until one of them, on the backward march, would allow his tail to double under him, and fall on his back, when they would immediately quit and scamper around like two madcaps. It was all done in the greatest good humour, and Sajo and Shapian never grew tired of watching them.

And between this uproarious exhibition, and the flute-playing, and the sword-swallowing, and the begging, the trundling around the wood and all the other racket and commotion that, on some days, only ceased when they went to sleep, they were about as busy, and noisy, and amusing a pair of little people as you could wish to live with.

But they were not always so lively. There came times when they were very quiet, when they would sit solemnly down together with their hands held tight to their chests and their tails before them, watching whatever was going on, still as two mice, looking, listening without a word, as though they were trying to make out what everything was all about. And sometimes, as they squatted there one beside the other, Sajo would kneel in front of them and tell them a story, marking time to the words with her finger before their noses, as though she were conducting an orchestra. And they would sit there and listen, and watch her finger very closely, and soon they would shake their heads up and down and from side to side, as beaver always do when they are pleased, and at last they would shake their whole bodies and their heads so hard that they would topple over and roll on the floor, exactly as if they had understood every word and just couldn't help laughing themselves to pieces over the story! And Shapian would stand by taking it all in, and finding it rather ridiculous; but at the same time he wished – very privately of couse – that he was not quite such a man, so he could join in this story-telling business himself. There were times when this thing of being grown-up rather interfered with the fun!

Sometimes the kittens were lonely, and would whimper together in their dark little home, and Sajo, who had never forgotten her own mother and knew why they were unhappy, would take them in her arms and croon softly to them, and try to comfort them. And they would snuggle up close to her, holding tight to each other's fur as though afraid to lose one another, and would bury their wee noses in the warm, soft spot in her neck where they so loved to be; and after a while the whimpering would cease and they would perhaps forget, for this time, and they would give big, long sighs and little moans of happiness, and fall asleep.

For, after all, with all their mischief and their shouting and their fun, they were just two small lost waifs, and they gave to these two human children, in their own humble way, the same love they had given to the father and the mother they had lost, and whom they never would forget.

Chikanee especially loved Sajo. Chikanee was not as strong as Chilawee, was quieter and more gentle. Chilawee had a rather jolly way about him, and was more of a roisterer, one of those "all for fun and fun for all" kind of lads to whom life is just one big joke; but Chikanee often

44

had lonely spells by himself, in corners, and had to be picked up, and petted, and made much of. Sometimes he came out in the night and cried beside Sajo's bed to be taken up and allowed to sleep there beside her – while Chilawee lay on his back below the bunk snoring away like a good fellow. When Chikanee was in some small trouble, such as bumping his nose on the stove, or getting the worst of a wrestling match, he came to Sajo for comfort. And Sajo, always ready to sympathise with him because he was the weaker of the two, would kneel down beside him on the floor; and then Chikanee would climb on to her lap and lie there, happy and contented. Chilawee, when his badness was all done for the day, and he was feeling perhaps a little left out of things, would come over to get *his* share of the petting, squeezing in tight beside Chikanee, where he would settle down after giving a few deep sighs, vastly pleased, no doubt, with his day's work. And Sajo, not wishing to disturb them, would stay there until they were ready to go.

It was very easy to tell them apart by now, as they had become quite different in their ways. Chilawee was stronger, bolder and more adventurous than his brother, a kind of a comical fellow who seemed to enjoy bumping his head on the table-legs, or dropping things on his toes, or falling into the woodbox. He was as inquisitive as a parrot and wanted to be into everything. Once he climbed up on to the edge of a pail of water that someone had left on the floor for a moment and, perhaps mistaking it for a plunge-hole, dived right into it. The pail, of course, upset with a bang, splashing the water in all directions. He was most surprised; and so was everybody else. But in spite of all this wilful behaviour, he was just as affectionate as Chikanee, and dogged Shapian's footsteps (when not otherwise engaged!) nearly as much as the other one did Sajo's. And he could not bear to be away from Chikanee very long. Everywhere they went they were together, trotting along one behind the other, or side by side, and if they should become parted on their wanderings in the camp, they would start out to look for each other, and call to one another. And when they met they would sit quite still for a little time, with their heads together, holding each other by the fur – though this wistful mood soon passed off, and it was not long before it all ended up in one of those queer wrestling matches, which seemed to be their way of celebrating.

And Sajo often thought how cruel it would be ever to part them.

CHAPTER SIX

THE TRADER

And then there came a time when Big Feather said that the kittens should be allowed their freedom. They were now quite a good size, and very active and strong, and the children were a little afraid that they would wander off and be forever lost. But their father told them how little beavers will not leave their home, if kindly treated, but would always return to the cabin as if it were a beaver house. He said they got lonely very quickly and would stay away only an hour or two.

So, one great, glorious and very exciting day, the barricade that had been kept across the bottom of the doorway was taken away, and out they went. Not all at once, though, for they did a lot of peeping and spying around corners, and sniffed and listened to a whole host of smells and sounds that were not really there at all, and they made two or three attempts before they finally ventured down to the lake, with Sajo and Shapian on either side for a bodyguard. They started off at a very slow and careful walk, sitting up every so often to look around for wolves and bears; of course there weren't any, but it was lots of fun pretending, and as they came closer to the lake the walk became faster, and broke into a trot, which soon became a gallop and into the water they rushed – and then dashed out again, hardly knowing what to make of so large a wash-tub as this. However, they soon went in again, and before very long were swimming, and diving, and screeching, and splashing their tails and having a glorious time, "Just like real beavers," said Sajo.

It wasn't long before they began to chew down small poplar saplings. These they cut into short lengths, and

47

peeled the bark off them in great enjoyment, while they sat among the tall grass and the rushes at the water's edge. They played and wrestled, and ran up and down the shore, and romped with their young human friends, and tore in and out of the water in a great state of mind. They stuck their inquisitive noses into every opening they saw, and found in the bank an empty muskrat hole. Being just about the same size as the muskrat, this suited them exactly, and they started to dig there. The opening was under water, and as they worked away there the mud began to come out in thick clouds, so that nothing in the water could be seen. And for a long time the beaver disappeared until, becoming alarmed, Shapian waded in and pushed his arm inside the hole and felt around. The beaver were not there! "Sajo," he called excitedly, "they are gone!" And the two of them hurriedly searched among the reeds and brush along the shore, when they heard behind them a most forlorn wailing and crying, and there, following them, running as fast as their stumpy little legs would carry them, came Chilawee and Chikanee, scared half to death for fear that they were being left behind. They had finished their work, and swimming under the muddy water, they had slipped away, and had landed further down the shore without being seen.

And now they were tired. So, sitting down like two little furry elves, they scrubbed, and rubbed, and combed their coats, and when that was done and they were quite dry, they turned and walked slowly and solemnly, side by side, up the pathway to the house. And there, with a big chunk of bannock apiece, they slipped quietly away into their birch-bark bedroom, and ate their lunch; and then, squeezing as tightly together as they could get on their nice, dry bed of shavings, fell fast asleep. And that was the end of their first great day of freedom.

At last they were, as Sajo had said, Real Beaver.

Every day after that, as soon as the door was opened,

they trotted down to the lake and had their daily swim. They spent hours at a time digging out the burrow they had found, and when it was far enough back to be safe, as they considered (you would have thought from the way they sometimes watched and snooped around, that the country was full of dragons), it was turned upwards and made to come out on top of the ground, and so become a plunge-hole, and over it, to the intense delight of Sajo and Shapian, they built a funny little beaver house! So now they had a real lodge, with a small room in it and an under-water entrance, a tunnel and a plunge-hole, all complete. The lodge was a little shaky about the walls, and was not very well plastered, but it was really quite a serviceable piece of work, considering.

Then they collected a quantity of saplings, and poplar and willow shoots, and made a tiny feed raft with them in front of their water-doorway, the same as grown-up beaver do, although it was ever so much smaller. Of course, all this feed would become sour in the water long before it could be used, and the summer was no time for feed-rafts, anyway, and the wobbly house could never keep out the rain; but little they cared! They had a warm bed of their own up in the cabin, same as the big folk had, and there was always plenty of bannock, and, on certain occasions, even a taste or two of preserves, and each had his own little dish to eat out of, so that, counting everything, they owned a considerable amount of property for the size of them and were really quite well-to-do. So they didn't need either the crazy-looking lodge or the feed-raft, but it was great fun fixing things up, and cutting little trees, and digging, and playing with mud (mud houses must be so much more interesting to make than mud pies!), and doing all those things that beaver like so much to do, and cannot live contentedly without.

Sajo and Shapian, who spent nearly all their time down there, were having just as good a time looking on, and often helped as well. Any building materials such as sticks, earth, or the odd stone that they brought down, were immediately pounced on by the two little beavers and carried away. And sometimes these young scalawags would come ashore covered with mud from head to foot, and try to climb all over their friends, and then there would be a regular scramble, and a great deal of laughter.

Shapian built a play-house by the water-side, and they were often all in there together, while they rested in the shade of it; and this was Chikanee's favourite spot, and he often went there to look for Sajo, and would always come there when she called him. But Chilawee, the adventurer, who was more of a rover, and something of a pirate, I'm inclined to think, could not stay still anywhere very long and would soon ramble away, and was continually getting lost. Of course *he* knew he wasn't lost, but the others thought he was, which amounted to the same thing so far as they were concerned; and then of course there would be a hunt. And he would turn up in the most unexpected places, and would be found in the play-house when it was supposed to be empty, or in the cabin when he was supposed to be in the play-house, or hidden away in the beaver lodge, or under the canoe, where he would be asleep as likely as not. And when found, he would sit upright with his tail out in front of him, and would teeter-totter and wiggle his body and shake his head, as if he were either dancing or laughing at the trick he had played on the rest of them. If there was a sudden and unreasonable commotion anywhere, it was nearly always safe to say that this scapegrace was at the bottom of it, and when there was any shouting, or squealing, or any kind of an uproar going on, Chilawee was always at his best – or his worst, whichever way you happened to look at it, and his voice could be heard calling from all kinds of places at all kinds of times.

Nor was Chikanee quite the saint you may begin to

think he was; he had as much fun as any of them. But there were times when he would break off quite suddenly, as though some thought had come into his head, perhaps some dim memory of his home-pond that was so far away among the Hills of the Whispering Leaves. And then, if Sajo were not there to comfort him, he would waddle on his squat little legs, up to the play-house to look for her. If he found her there, he would sit beside her and wash himself; and after he was all tidied up, he would nestle close to this so-well-loved companion. With his head on her knee, he would try to talk to her in his queer beaver language and tell her what the trouble was; or else lie there with his eyes half closed and dreamy, making small sounds of happiness, or perhaps of love – we cannot know. Very, very good friends indeed were these two, and where one was, there would be the other, before very long.

And what with all the lively antics, and the skylarking, and the work (not too much of it of course) and all the play, it would be hard for me to tell you just who were the happiest among these youngsters, those with four legs, or those with two. But this I *do* know, that they were a very merry crew, in those happy, happy days at O-pee-pee-soway, The Place of Talking Waters.

The titbits of bannock had been getting smaller and smaller lately. Big Feather had been away some days now for more provisions, and had not yet returned, and now there was hardly any flour. Nobody, children or beaver, had very much to eat, until one day the four of them arrived back at the cabin to find Gitchie Meegwon there.

He looked very grave and troubled about something. But the provisions were there; a bag of flour and some other goods lay on the floor, and beside them stood a white man, a stranger. This man had with him a large box. Big Feather spoke kindly to his children, but he never smiled as he generally did, and they wondered why. The white man, too, stood there without speaking. Somehow things didn't look right. Even the little beaver seemed to feel that there was something amiss, for animals are often quick to feel such things, and they, too, stood there quietly, watching.

And Shapian, who had been to Mission School and understood English fairly well, heard his father say to the man: "There they are; which one are you going to take?"

What was that! What could he mean? With a sudden sick feeling Shapian looked at his sister; but of course she had not understood.

"Wait till I have a look at them," said the stranger, answering Big Feather's question. "Let them move around a bit." He was a stout, red-faced man with hard blue eyes – like glass, or ice, thought Shapian. But Big Feather's eyes were sad, as he looked at his boy and girl. He asked the white man to wait a moment, while he spoke to his children.

"Sajo, Shapian; my daugher, my son," he said in Indian, "I have something to tell you."

Sajo knew then that some trouble had come to them. She came close to Shapian, and looked timidly at the stranger – why, oh why, was he looking so hard at the beaver!

"Children," continued their father, "this is the new trader, from the fur-post at Rabbit Portage; the old one, our good friend, has gone. A new Company has taken over the post, and they ask me to pay my debt. It is a big debt, and cannot be paid until we make our hunt, next winter. The other Company always dealt that way with the Indians. But the new Company say they cannot wait. We now have no provisions, as you know, and this Company will give me nothing until the debt is paid. So I must go on a long journey for them, with the other men of the village, moving supplies to the new post at Meadow Lake, which is far from here. My work will pay the debt, and more, but I will receive no money until I return. In the meantime, you my children, must live. I cannot see you go hungry. This trader will give us these provisions." Here he pointed at the bags and parcels lying on the floor. "And in exchange he wants – he wants one of the beaver." He stopped, and no one so much as moved, not even the beaver, and he continued, "Live beaver are very valuable, and whichever one he takes will not be killed. But my heart is heavy for you, my children, and –" he looked at Chilawee and Chikanee, "and for the little beaver that must go."

Shapian stood very still and straight, his black eyes looking hard at the trader, while Sajo, hardly believing, whispered, "It isn't true; oh, it isn't true!"

But Shapian never spoke, only put his arm around his sister's shoulder, and stared hard at this man, this stranger who had come to spoil their happiness. He thought of his loaded gun, so close behind him in the corner; but his father must be obeyed, and he never moved. And he looked so fiercely at the trader that, although he was only a fourteen-year-old boy, the man began to feel a little uneasy; so he opened his box, and reaching out for one of the beaver, picked the little fellow up, put him in it and shut down the lid. He nodded to Gitchie Meegwon:

"Well, I'll be seeing you down at the post in a couple of days," he said, and walked out with the box under his arm, shutting the door behind him.

Just like that.

And then Sajo, without a sound, fell to her knees beside her brother and buried her face in his sleeve.

The trader had chosen Chikanee.

And Chilawee, not knowing what to think, suddenly afraid, went into his little cabin, alone.

53

CHAPTER SEVEN

SAJO HEARS THE TALKING WATERS

The next day Big Feather started away for the fur-post, on his way to work out his debt to the Company. With him were seventeen other men from the village, in three big bark canoes. At Rabbit Portage they would load up the canoes with supplies for Meadow Lake, or Muskodasing, another of the Company's posts, far to the north. The brigade, as such canoe caravans are called, would be gone a month or more. And Sajo, Shapian, and Chilawee were left alone at O-pee-pee-soway.

When the trader had so sharply shut the door between her and the one thing, next to her father and her brother, she loved most in all the world, it had seemed to Sajo as if the door had closed on her heart as well, and that it too had gone out with Chikanee, in the box.

After this, a big change had come over all three of them. The happy circle had been broken up. There were no more merry parties in the play-house, no more fun or laughter on the lake shore. Chilawee cut no capers any more, and his voice, that used to be heard at all times and everywhere, was still. He never did his funny, jolly dance and never played, but wandered miserably up and down the water-trail all the day long, searching for Chikanee. He couldn't seem to get it into his head that his brother was gone. He would start out fresh and hopeful every morning, at a little trot, feeling sure that he would find him somewhere, looking in every corner of the play-house, and running from one to another of the trampled places in the grass and reeds, where they had so often sat together and combed themselves, and wrestled, and basked in the sunlight side by side. He swam up and down

54

along the shore, searching at all their old landing-places, and dived in and out of the shaky little lodge that it had been such fun to build.

So he hunted all day, until at last he would give up, and his eager, shuffling trot would become a slow and weary walk, and he plodded on his tired little legs up the pathway to the camp and lay, without a sound, in his empty, silent hut – no longer a rollicking pirate, no more a mischievous scapegrace, but just a lonely, sorrowful little beaver. He was not Big Small any more, just Small, because now he was all the Small there was. The two children followed him on his rounds, and pretended they were looking too, though they knew his search was useless; for they could not bear to see him haunting around all by himself, like an unhappy little ghost. And when he ate from his dish they both sat down beside him and held it for him; and sometimes there would be one or two big tears fall into the bread and milk when Sajo thought of Chikanee, who should have been there too – poor Chikanee, poor Little Small who had been so soft and gentle and who had often been so lonely, now away somewhere in the great city, where there was no more romping, no more bannock, no more fun!

Somehow, it seemed that he couldn't be really gone. Sajo more than half expected to find the squat little figure sitting somewhere in the play-house, or to see a short-legged dumpy little body come bouncing out beside Chilawee from the birch-bark cabin for his daily feast of bannock, and almost any minute she was ready to declare that she had heard his voice down at the landing. Even his little tracks, much smaller than Chilawee's, ugly, turned-in and pathetic, were still there in the mud beside the water. Sajo would go very often to look at them, and when no one was near, she knelt down and touched them gently with her fingers, and whispered to them; until at last they were washed away and disappeared. Over the very last one that was left, she laid a sheet of birch bark, and every day made a visit to it, alone; but even it gradually dried out, and faded to dust, and was soon quite gone.

And then there was nothing left of him at all.

Though Chilawee's voice was seldom heard these days, yet sometimes in the night he awoke and, whimpering in utter loneliness, groped in the darkness for another small round body that he could never find. And Sajo would hear him and awaken, and would creep under the bunk and lie beside him on his little bed of shavings and hold him close to her, sobbing, until they both would fall asleep again.

Shapian sat for hours looking out over the lake, staring across at the far-away, for ever marching hill, saying nothing, his heart aching for his sister, who never sang or laughed around the cabin any more, as she had used to do. How he hated those bags and parcels the trader had exchanged for Chikanee! The bannock nearly choked him when he ate it. If only he had thought to offer the trader his gun; four mink skins it had cost, and surely they were worth as much as one small, very small kitten beaver!

Although they had shared their pets, and Chilawee was really his, Shapian gave him up entirely to his sister. And she would sometimes take the little beaver, and carry him quite a distance up a creek that came tumbling down from out the hills behind the village, to where there was a low waterfall. Beside the fall there was a great, whispering pine tree, and there, beneath the tree, she would sit and try to think of some way to get Chikanee back, while Chilawee swam, and dived, and even played a little by himself, in the quiet, deep pool below. He seemed happier there, Sajo thought, because the pool was small, and did not seem so wide and empty as did the lake, with its miles and miles of distance all around and only one small beaver there to fill it up.

And while her small companion swam around, or

peeled his willow sticks, and sometimes sat upon her lap and combed himself, she would listen to the voices in the falls. For, you must know, if you wait very patiently beside a rapids or a waterfall, you seem to hear, after a time, the sound of low murmuring voices, voices that come and go, now louder, now softer, sometimes seeming quite distinct, then fading away to be lost again in the muttering of the water. All Indians have heard these sounds, and white people who have listened say they too can hear them, soft and singing in the brook. The Indians say that these are the voices of people from the Spirit Land, come back to speak to those they love. And here Sajo would sit until the voices came, and try to make out what they were saying. She was sure that some day she would be able to understand them, which was indeed likely, because Indian language so much resembles the sound of running water, the sighing of the wind, and the whispering of the trees. And Chilawee often sat beside her very quietly, as if he were listening, and perhaps he heard them too, better even than Sajo did, for a beaver's ears are much sharper than a man's.

This was the spot that the Indians called O-pee-pee-soway, The Place of Talking Waters, for which the village and the country round about was named. It had been Sajo's favourite place ever since she had been a very little girl, whenever she wanted to think, or make up her mind about something. Often she would lie in the shade of the great pine, looking up into the dark, shadowy caverns between the giant branches; and she sometimes wondered if that was where the spirits lived who spoke to people from the Talking Water. And as she lay gazing up into the gently swaying pine-top, listening to the stream, she used to feel somehow that her mother was near, speaking to her; and this made her very happy.

One day, as she sat there with Chilawee in her lap, listening to the drowsy murmur of the little fall, the sounds seemed to become very clear and plain, and she leaned back against the tree and shut her eyes, so as to hear them better. And after a while the sound of the water became less and less, and soon died quite away; and she thought that she could hear in place of it, someone speaking very softly, very plainly there beside her. And soon she began to make out the words, and the words were in the Indian language, that sounds so much like running water: Over and over again she heard the words repeated, like a rhyme of poetry, or a song.

> "Sajo, Sajo,
> Mah-jahn, mah-jahn.
> Sajo, Sajo,
> 'Den-na jah-dahn."

> "Sajo, Sajo,
> You must go.
> To the city
> You must go."

On and on the voice seemed to chant these words, now louder, now softer, the sound coming and going as the murmur of the water in the falls had done. And it became so plain at last, that she even seemed to recognize the voice, a voice she had not heard for so long – her mother's voice. And she cried:

"Oh my mother, here is Sajo. Oh my mother, tell me more. I will listen to the words you tell me." And she reached out towards the sound and touched something soft and warm, as she opened her eyes rather suddenly to find her hand on the warm, damp nose of Chilawee, who was sitting up on her lap, pulling at her head-shawl. She knew then that she had, for a moment, been asleep; and the words were lost again in the singing of the water, and the falls murmured on and on as they had always done.

Then Sajo jumped to her feet and took Chilawee up, and said to him: "Chilawee, Chilawee, we are going to get Chikanee; we must go to the city for Chikanee. My mother has told me. I *know*."

So, carrying the little beaver in her arms, she started to run back home, and as she ran she said to herself: yes, it was the voice of my mother. The Great Spirit let her come to the waterfall and speak to me; and she told me to go to the city – just wait till I tell Shapian!

Meanwhile Chilawee got all shaken up with the running and didn't like it a bit, and he struggled to get down, and cried out at the top of his voice, as he had not done for many a long day. And Sajo thought: he's got his voice back again, just as before Chikanee went away, and that means my dream will come true. I *know* it will; and she ran so much the harder. And between the running of one, and the calling out of the other, both of them were pretty well out of breath when they arrived at the cabin. And Shapian, seeing them in this state, came quickly out of the door and asked what the matter was; and Sajo told him of her dream and how they must certainly go to the city.

But Shapian was not so ready to agree; he hadn't yet had time to think it over, and besides he hadn't had any dream. So he said: "This is foolish, my sister; the city is far, we don't know the way, we have no money, and without money we can get neither bed nor food there; besides, we would have to take Chilawee. And what would our father say?"

This all sounded very discouraging, but Sajo was not to be so easily turned aside, once she had made up her mind, and she answered: "Our father is as sorry as we are, and would be glad if we found Chikanee again; for none of us has been happy since he was taken away."

But she said nothing about how she thought they were going to get to the city, or about what they would do if they did get there. For she believed very firmly in the

message she had heard, and was quite positive that
something wonderful was bound to come of it. And
Shapian looked at his sister and saw how her eyes were
shining with hope. To do as she asked would be hard, he
knew – the hardest thing he had ever tried; but to refuse,
without even trying, and then to see her more broken-
hearted than ever, would be harder yet. And his father
had told him, before he left, to do all he could to make her
happy once again. So, "Yes," he said, "we will go." And
he stood up very straight, in the way he had, and looked
very firm and manly. "Yes. I will take you to the city.
Tomorrow."

But for all he looked so stern and proud, Shapian had
not the faintest idea of how he was going to set about it,
nor did he ever guess how desperate an adventure this
would turn out to be.

CHAPTER EIGHT

THE RED ENEMY

Late the same night everything was in readiness for the journey. It would take them many days to reach the trading post at Rabbit Portage, the first step of their long journey to the city; and they had no idea what lay beyond the post. So they took plenty of everything that was needed for a long trip. Sajo had made several large bannocks, and filled different sized canvas bags with flour, tea and salt. She made up a parcel of dried deer meat, set aside a small pail of lard and put matches in a tight-topped can where they would remain dry. Shapian was not idle. He rolled up a tent and blankets, fixed up a fishing line, sharpened a belt-axe and his hunting-knife, whittled a thin edge on the blades of the paddles, and boxed up whatever pots and dishes they would have need of.

The sun had not yet arisen on the following morning when breakfast was over and the full outfit was loaded in the canoe, along with Shapian's rifle; for much as he prized this gun, he intended to sell it if he could, hoping that it would bring at least enough to pay their way to the city. What was to happen after that he didn't dare even to think about. Chilawee went in the same birch-bark basket in which he and Chikanee had first come to O-pee-pee-soway, and in the cookery-box Sajo had put *both* the little beaver dishes, as this helped her to feel more certain that they were going to bring back Chikanee and Chilawee together.

"We will need them both," she said aloud, "for" – and here her voice dropped a little – "we *are* going to get him, I think," and then louder, as she nodded her head and

61

pursed her lips, "I just *know* we are." And to make her belief the stronger she added, "My mother said so. In the sound of Mudway-oshkay I heard her; in the sounding of the water she has told me!"

You see, her dream seemed so very real, and meant so much to her.

The village was some distance away from their cabin, and they had told no one about their plans, for fear the older people might try to stop them. The old Chief, especially, might forbid them. So they slipped away into the mists of early morning without anyone being the wiser. And as they floated out from the landing, Sajo shook her paddle above her head, as she had seen the men do when they started on a journey, shouting the name of the place they were bound for; and so she held her paddle up and cried out "Chik-a-*nee*! Chik-a-*nee*!" You could hardly call Chikanee a place, but, she thought, wherever he is, that's where we are going. But Shapian did not wave his paddle, nor did he shout; for he was not so sure about where they would end up.

And so they left the Place of Talking Waters, and started out on what was to be, for all three of them, their Great Adventure.

The canoe was the one with the eye and the tail, the one which Gitchie Meegwon had used on the River of Yellow Birches, and in it they paddled swiftly all that day, the great eye staring eagerly ahead and the fox's tail fluttering gaily out behind. They stopped occasionally in order to put Chilawee over the side to have a drink and swim around for a minute or two so as to get cooled off, for the weather was very hot; and that evening they put up their tent in the woods along the shore, and spent the night there. The next morning at daybreak they were away again, and paddled steadily till dark, stopping only to eat and to exercise Chilawee. Each morning they were on their feet before the sun rose, and every evening they made

62

camp in some sheltered spot beside the water, where Chilawee swam around all night, returning to the tent at daylight to fall asleep in his basket, where he remained quietly all day. Both Sajo and Shapian worked the portages, when they had to walk, lifting the canoe out of the water and taking a well-marked trail to avoid waterfalls or dangerous rapids. It took two journeys each to transport all their goods, including the canoe, which was light enough for Shapian to carry on his own. Neither of them found this to be particularly hard work, for that kind of journey was nothing new to either of them.

And so day after day they forged ahead, onward, onward, ever onward; and two small backs bent and swayed like clockwork and two paddles swished and dipped all the long day, as regularly and evenly as the step of marching soldiers, while the burning sun rose on one side of them, passed overhead, and sank again like a great red ball behind the dark wall of the forest. Day after day the faithful bark canoe carried them staunchly and steadily forward, outward bound on the long search for the absent Chikanee.

And in all that great wilderness they were just a little moving speck that crawled across the silver surface of wide, boundless lakes, alone on the face of all the world; but it was a speck that held two brave young people, one of whom, at least, who was full of hope – and another young creature who was full of bannock and who lay snoring contentedly, even if not too happily in his basket.

One morning they awoke to a faint smell of wood-smoke in the air, a smell of burning moss and scorching brush and leaves, and they knew that somewhere, seemingly far away, there was a forest fire. But it was closer then they had at first supposed, for as soon as they were well out on the lake and were able to look about them, they could see an immense pillar of smoke billowing up from behind the distant hills; and they did not paddle very far before they found that their route would bring them more and more in its direction. The lake was getting very narrow, and farther on it ended and became a river, across which the fire could easily jump, and Shapian determined to get through this narrow place as quickly as possible, to a large lake that lay beyond, where they would be safe. So they hurried on, and as they went the smoke spread higher and wider, so that it was no longer a pillar, but a white wall that seemed to reach the sky, and rolled outwards and down in all directions, becoming thicker and thicker until the sun was hidden, and the air became heavy and stifling, and very still. The whole country to the east seemed to be on fire, and although the blaze itself was hidden by the hills, even at that distance there could be heard a low moaning sound that never ceased and was, minute by minute, becoming closer – they were right in the path of the fire. The big lake was some distance away, across a portage, and there was no time to be lost if they were to cross over to it before the fire rushed down upon them; for some forest fires have been known to travel as fast as thirty miles an hour.

As the hot smoke cooled off, it began to come down, setting in a dark, blue haze over all the land, making far-off points invisible and near ones look dim, so that soon nothing could be seen but the row of trees nearest the shore-line, and they were only able to keep their right direction by watching this, and by the sound of the rapids that lay ahead of them. Very soon they arrived at the head of this steep place in the river, where the water rushed and foamed wildly between, and over, dark jagged rocks for several hundred metres. It was a dangerous place, but Shapian dared not allow the time which the double trip required to use the portage trail that went around it. He decided to take the quicker route and run the rapids. For the fire was now not far away, and the sharp turn that he knew to be at the end of the swift water would head them straight for it. The roar of the fire was now so loud as almost to drown the sound of the noisy rapids, and Shapian soon saw that it was to be a hard race, and a swift one, to gain the lake – and then there was the portage, and it was a long one.

The smoke was now so thick that when they neared the rapids they could not see twelve metres ahead of them, and Shapian had all he could do to find the way. Standing up in the canoe to get a better view, he at length found the starting point; and then with a swift rush they were into the dashing, boiling white water. Although he was hardly able to see through the smoke, Shapian skilfully picked his way down the crooked, difficult channel between the rocks. Great curling, hissing waves lashed out at the frail canoe, throwing it violently from one white-cap to another; dark, oily-looking swells gripped its under-side like evil monsters seeking to pour it over the sides and sink it. Spinning eddies snatched wickedly at the paddles as the little craft leaped like a madly charging horse between the black, savage-looking rocks that lay in wait to rip and tear the light canoe to pieces.

And above the thunderous roar of the tumbling waters there came the duller, deeper, and terribly frightening sound of the oncoming fire. Smoke poured across the river in dense, whirling clouds, and through it sped the leaping canoe with its crew of three. And the sleeping passenger in the basket woke up, and excited by all the noise, and quite aware that something unusual was happening, began to take a part in the proceedings, and added his little thin voice to the uproar, though it could hardly be heard, and he rocked and shook his house of bark so violently that a moment had to be spared to lay a heavy bundle on it to keep it right side up.

Shapian strained and fought with his paddle and all of his strength, against the mighty power of the racing torrent, turning the canoe cleverly this way and that, swinging, sidling, and slipping from one piece of clear water to the next, checking the canoe in the quieter places while he stood up to get a better view of what lay ahead – and then away into the white water again. Meanwhile Sajo pulled and pushed on her paddle with might and main, as Shapian shouted instructions to her above the rattle and the din. Sheets of spray flew from the sides of the canoe as it heaved and bounced and jerked, and some of it came in, and Sajo, who was in front, soon became soaked. Except that the smoke made the safe channel so hard to find, they were in no real danger from the rapids itself, for Shapian, like all his people was very skilful in a canoe and understood, even at his age, a great deal about the movements of water; and he had often run these rapids with his father. Sajo, trusting in him completely, laughed and cried out in her excitement, for this was like a show to her, and she let out little yelps as she had heard her father and the other Indians do as they ran a dangerous piece of water – though she had always been left safely on the shore to watch. But Shapian, who knew how serious things really were, never made a sound besides his loud commands, and when he could spare an eye from the turmoil of madly boiling water all about him, gave anxious glances to the side from which the fire was coming. And coming it was – with the speed of a train, it seemed – rushing down the hills towards them like a crimson sea, with great roaring streamers of flame flying high above the burning forest. Once he looked back, to find that the fire had crossed the narrow lake behind them; now there was only one way to go – forward. The air, that had been thick with heavy rolls and banks of smoke, now began to turn darker and darker, and the light was dimmed till it appeared almost as though twilight had fallen. Hardly anything could be seen around them; and nothing seemed real any more, and they moved like people in a dream.

Desperately Shapian drove the canoe ahead, for well he knew that if they were caught in this place they would be either burnt alive or suffocated. By now the portage was not very far, and beyond it lay the lake that they must get to — and get to fast!

They shot out from the foot of the rapids into a deep, still pool, and here they found themselves surrounded by strange moving shapes, dimly seen through the smoke-clouds, as all manner of animals were passing, tearing along the shore, or swimming through the pool, or splashing noisily along the shallows, by ones and twos, separately or in small groups, all headed for the big lake, each and every one making for the safety that he knew he would find there. Animals that seldom wetted their feet were swimming in the pool – squirrels, rabbits, wood-chucks, and even porcupines. Deer leaped through or over the underbrush, their white tails flashing, eyes wide with terror. A bear lumbered by at a swift, clumsy gallop, and a pair of wolves ran, easily and gracefully, beside a deer – their natural prey; but they never even looked at him. For none were enemies now; no one was hungry, or fierce, or afraid of another. And all the people of the woods, those that went on two legs and others that had four, and those with wings and some that swam, animals and birds and creeping things, creatures, some of them, that dared not meet at any other time, were now fleeing, side by side, from that most merciless of all their foes, dangerous and deadly alike to every one of them from the smallest to the greatest – the Red Enemy of the Wilderness, a forest fire.

Right before the canoe, deep in the water, stood a giant bull moose, largest of all the forest animals, his hair scorched from his back, one of his half-grown horns gone, his sides heaving as he sucked in great, deep breaths of air; he must have been nearly caught, and perhaps had run many miles with the fire close behind him, and had only escaped because of his enormous strength and speed. Shapian could have touched him with his paddle had he wished, but the huge beast paid them no attention and, getting his wind again, plunged ashore and joined the other creatures of all shapes and sizes that, brothers now in this great calamity, were hurrying together to the safety of the lake.

And with them, in this wild and queer procession, were two little Indians and their tiny pet.

Sajo, now realizing what all this meant, became terror-stricken, and Shapian, almost in despair himself, yet knowing that their lives depended on him, kept up his courage and soothed her as best he could, and she paddled bravely on. But the forest that had always been their home, and had always seemed so friendly, had suddenly become a very terrible place to be in. It would have been so to any grown-up; yet these two, one of them eleven and the other fourteen, kept their heads and fought for their lives, and for Chilawee's. And this same Chilawee was no great help, on the contrary, he showed every sign of causing trouble and delay. Sensing real danger, as all animals do, and scared out of his wits by the sounds and scent of the other creatures that passed on every side, he was screeching at the top of his lungs and pounding and tearing at the lid of his prison, as it must now have seemed to him. If some way were not found to quiet him, he would soon be out of it; and once in the water he could never again be found in all this hurry and confusion.

A few short minutes and they were at the portage. The trail was nearly hidden by the blinding smoke, and down the slopes of the near-by ridge the hoarse roar of the fire was coming swiftly. The darkness that had fallen as the smoke poured over the forest was now lighted up by a terrible red glow, and the heat from it could be plainly felt. Quickly they threw their stuff ashore. Chilawee was now in such a state that he could not be carried except as a

68

separate load. This landing being safe for the minute, and knowing what shape things were in at the other end, they at once decided to leave him. It was but the work of a moment to turn the canoe over on top of the basket, so as to hold down the lid, and each taking a load they started across, running at a dog-trot. On all sides thick moving coils of black and yellow smoke wound and billowed around them as they ran, and took strange shapes and forms and seemed to reach out with pale waving hands to hold them back, and through the whirling smoke-clouds the trees beside the trail loomed indistinct like tall, dark, silent ghosts; while here and there red eyes of flame glowed at them through the haze.

But they kept right on at their steady trot. At the far side there was a breeze from off the lake, and the end of the portage was clear. Gulping a few breaths of fresh air, they left their loads beside the water's edge and raced back for Chilawee and the canoe – I say "raced," but the race was often little but a scramble as, gasping and half blinded, they staggered down the trail, half the time with their eyes closed to relieve the pain in them, and to shut out the stinging, burning smoke, while they groped their way along, their hearts filled with a fear such as they had never before known. By the time they were back at the canoe, sparks and burning brands were falling every- where, and the angry glow had deepened so that everything – trees, smoke, and water – was red with it. And now, close at hand, could be heard a dreadful low, rushing sound.

The fire was almost upon them.

And at the same time Chilawee, having made up his mind to save his own little life as best he could, was gnawing steadily away at the thin bark sides of his box; in no time at all he would be through. If only it would hold together for just five more minutes!

In a moment Shapian tore off his sister's head-shawl,

and quickly soaking it in water, with swift movements wrapped it about her head and face, leaving only her eyes and nose showing. Then, splashing water over her clothes he said: "Do not wait. I will come quickly. Go!"

And hugging Chilawee's basket tight to her body with both arms, Sajo disappeared into that awful, glowing tunnel of a trail.

CHAPTER NINE

THE EMPTY BASKET

After he had seen his sister pass from sight, Shapian was delayed perhaps a full minute while he wetted his own clothes and slipped the paddles into the carrying-thongs. How he wished now for his father's guiding hand! He was doing the best he knew, with his small experience, to save the lives of all three of them (for he looked on the little beaver almost as though he, too, were a person, a little brother who must be saved as well) and he hoped he had chosen aright. And now Sajo was in there ahead of him, alone; he must hurry!

Throwing the canoe up and over, with his head inside between the paddles, which formed a kind of yoke, he was quickly on his way. But in that short minute that he had been detained, the fire had gained on him, and while he ran as swiftly as a boy of fourteen could well do with a birch-bark canoe on his shoulders, he saw, not far away to one side, a solid, crackling wall of flame. Trees fell crashing in the midst of it, and others burst with loud reports like gun-fire. Onward he tore through what had now become a cave of crimson smoke, half-choked, his eyes stinging, his head throbbing with the heat. But he clenched his teeth and kept on, while close beside him the blazing forest crackled, and thundered, and roared. Whole tree-tops caught fire with a rush and a horrible screeching, tearing sound, and flames leaped from tree to tree like fiery banners, ever nearer and nearer to the trail.

Beneath the canoe some clear air remained, which helped him a little, but the heat was as much as he could stand. Once a burning spruce tree came crashing down so near the portage that its flaming top fell across the trail

71

ahead of him, and he was obliged to wait precious moments while the first fury of the burning brush died down; and then he jumped, with the canoe still on his shoulders, over the glowing trunk. The hot breath of it fanned his body and nearly choked him, and he stumbled as he landed. Righting himself, he cleared the canoe before the fire had harmed it, but the bravely flying fox tail had caught on fire, and in a moment was scorched to a crisp. But he went on.

On the upturned canoe fell large flakes of burning bark and red-hot ashes that lay there and smoked and smouldered, so that to anyone who might have followed him, it must have seemed to be already burning, which, in very truth, it was not far from doing. And now he should have caught up to his sister; she would be slower than he, for the basket was an awkward shape to run with, whereas a bark canoe, though very much heavier, was a steady, well-balanced load. And he suddenly became terrified lest Chilawee had cut open his box and escaped on the way, and Sajo had delayed somewhere to capture him, and so he had passed them. But just ahead the smoke was clearing, and he felt the wind from the lake. And then, sick and dizzy, his sight blurred by the water that streamed from his eyes, he stumbled again, and this time fell heavily, canoe and all, over something soft that lay in the pathway. It was Sajo, who lay face down across the trail! And clutched tightly in one of her hands was the basket – empty. Chilawee had at last cut his way out, and was gone!

Hardly knowing what he was doing, Shapian crawled from under the canoe, lifted Sajo across his knees and scrambled, somehow, to his feet. Then, his breath coming in choking sobs, his knees bending under him and a great ringing in his ears, he staggered with her in his arms to the lake shore.

Here he laid her down and threw water over her face,

and rubbed her hands, and cried out, "Sajo, Sajo, speak to me, speak!" And she opened her eyes and said faintly, "Chilawee." And he dared not tell her there was no Chilawee any more, only an empty basket.

And now the smoke was rolling out over them even here; the whole portage was aflame. Waiting only to wet Sajo's shawl and throw it over her face, Shapian went back for the canoe. Fortunately it was not far as, unable to lift it any more, he seized it by one end and dragged it to the water, stern out and bow inshore so as to load all the quicker. Swiftly he threw in the bundles and lifted Sajo into the bow. She still clung tightly to the basket and cried weakly, "Chilawee, Chilawee, Chilawee."

All this took but a short time and, running lightly over the load to the other end, Shapian began to back out the canoe stern first, as fast as he was able; and a big sob came in his throat as he thought of their furry friend who was now past all help, left behind. Yet surely, he thought, the little creature, gifted to find water so easily, might have reached the lake, and even if lost might still be living – when behind him, from the lake, came the sound of a smart slap, and there was the lost Chilawee! Not only was he alive and quite well, thank you, but he was giving out, by means of his tail, his private and personal opinion of this Red Enemy that he had so narrowly escaped. And Shapian shouted out in a great voice: "Sajo! Sajo! Chilawee is safe, Chilawee is out on the lake – look!"

And at that Sajo, lying there in the bow of the canoe, burst into tears and sobbed as if her heart would break; she would not cry before, when she believed her little friend was dead, but now he was known to be safe she was free to cry all she wanted, to cry as loud and as long as she liked – with joy!

Chilawee was quite far out, and in no danger, but a canoe does not start very quickly when paddled backwards, and it was too close to shore for safety. For at

73

the edge of the forest, leaning out over the water, was a huge pine tree that was hollow, and had been burning fiercely all this time. Shapian was still struggling to get the canoe backed away far enough to turn it (and it did not take nearly as long for all this to happen as it does to tell about it), when the bark of the pine, dried out by the intense heat, cracked wide open, and a tongue of fire rushed up this channel as if it had been a stove-pipe, to the top of it. The great fan-shaped head of the towering tree, that had looked proudly out over the wilderness for many a hundred years, burst into a mass of flame that leaped into the air above it, the height again of the tree itself. And then the burnt-out butt, unable to stand against the force of the soaring flames, gave way, and the mighty trunk tottered and began to fall, outwards towards the lake, swayed a little sideways, and then started on its fiery path, straight for the canoe. Slowly at first, then faster and faster the giant overbalanced, and the terrible fan of flame rushed downwards. Real terror, for the first time, seized on Shapian, and with desperate strength he stopped the canoe and drove it smashing into the shore, while just behind him the burning tree plunged into the lake with a deafening crash, and a hissing and a screeching that could have been heard for a mile or more as fire and water met. Smoke and steam poured up and smothered everything, so that Shapian could see nothing, and the waves from this terrific splash rocked the canoe violently. Sajo, beside herself with fright, jumped to her feet in the dangerously rolling canoe and screamed, and screamed, and Shapian sprang over the side and ran through the water to her, and held her in his arms, and comforted her, and told her that there was nothing more to fear.

And out on the lake Chilawee slapped his little tail in small defiance; or perhaps it was intended for an imitation of the falling tree – in which case it was a pretty feeble imitation!

In a few short moments the canoe was away, this time without any accident, and the little beaver gave himself up quite cheerfully, and was lifted by this so-impudent tail of his and dropped aboard where he clambered around on the load, and sniffed at the children, and ran about, and altogether showed signs of the greatest pleasure and excitement. He did not seem to have lost one single hair, no doubt because he ran so low to the ground on his short legs, so that everything passed over him; and so now he was celebrating, and they all had quite a reunion out there on the lake.

Before they had gone very far, Sajo began to feel better, and soon was well enough to sit up. Shapian would not let her paddle, and made her sit facing him, while she told her story, and related how, choked by the hot, burning smoke, and not being able to see, she had been unable to catch Chilawee when he fell from the basket, and had become confused and fallen, where, she did not know, and had then been unable to get up again. And that was all she knew about it until she found Shapian pouring water over her face. She did not remember calling Chilawee, though she knew he had run away, having seen him, as though in a dream, disappear into the clouds of smoke. And when she had finished her story, she began to look hard at her brother's face, and then began to laugh! The more she looked the louder she laughed, and Shapian was a little frightened, and began to wonder if the dangers she had been through had touched her mind, until she exclaimed: "Shapian! Your face – you should see it, why – you have no eyebrows!" Then suddenly she stopped laughing and felt for her own eyebrows, and asked anxiously: "How are mine, are they all right?" and looked over the side of the canoe at the water to see the reflection of her face. But the canoe was moving, and ruffling the water, and she could, of course, see nothing, and now very alarmed she cried: "Oh, stop the canoe so I can see – tell me, are my eyebrows there?"

And she got into a great way about it, and Shapian laughed at her, in his turn, and would not say; until at last he told her they were there all right, yes, both of them; which indeed they were, as her face had been covered most of the time. But it was just like a girl, said Shapian to himself, to worry about a little thing like eyebrows when they had all so nearly lost their lives!

The canoe had suffered most, and was leaking rather badly, but otherwise everything was going quite smoothly again. But behind them the fire swept over the portage and on beyond it, like a conquering army, leaving everything in its path a blackened, smoking ruin. Well, they were safe now, and except for two aching heads and two pairs of smarting eyes, were in the best of spirits. Shapian, for once, felt quite encouraged at having beaten the fire, because, as Sajo put it, there was hardly *anything* worse to be met with than a forest fire, and they had come right *through* it (as she imagined), so nothing in the world could *ever* keep them now from Chikanee. As for Chilawee, he appeared to have come through the affair the best of any of them, and evidently gave the matter no further thought; and stretching himself out on the bottom of the canoe, with his head comfortably pillowed on Sajo's knee, he promptly went to sleep.

That afternoon they made an early camp, in a good safe place, on an island far out on the lake, and here they looked over the damage. Shapian could not very well repair his eyebrows, which would grow out later of their own accord, but he had plenty to do with the canoe. The gallant tail was just a blackened, shrivelled piece of skin, and the once-keen, watchful eye was nearly gone, most of the paint having blistered, and cracked, and fallen off. The hard smash the bow had got against the shore when they had dodged the falling tree had torn off a good-sized strip of bark; the spruce-gum at the seams had melted, and the burning embers that had fallen on it had smouldered long enough to scorch a number of pretty thin places in the sides and bottom. Also their tent and blankets had a few holes burnt in them by flying sparks. But the loss was quite small, considering, and they could easily have fared a great deal worse. The top was gone off Chilawee's box, and it had a hole the size of a fist in the side of it (Chilawee's part in the battle!). But there were plenty of birch trees around, and Shapian cut sheets of bark from them, and sewed a patch on the hole and made another lid that fitted nearly as well as the old one, and he fixed up the canoe with a few patches and some fresh gum. The eye and the tail would have to wait until later. Sajo, meanwhile, busied herself with needle and thread which no Indian girl or woman will travel very far without, and soon had the tent and blankets serviceable again, and by the time darkness fell, everything was in readiness for a new start in the morning.

And that night, as the two of them sat side by side, looking across to the mainland, they were thinking how nearly they had come to never seeing their father again, and they longed for him. And they could hear, even yet, faintly in the distance, the low moaning of the fire, while the sky shone red for many miles, lit up by the beautiful, but terrible glow from that greatest of all dangers of the Wilderness. They knew that great forests, and thousands of animals, and often whole towns full of people, have been destroyed by a single match in the hands of one careless man.

Later, as Shapian lay on his bed of brush, watching the slow fading of the red glow on the canvas walls of the tent, he came to the very pleasing conclusion that even if he were not really yet a man, at this rate of going it would not be very long before he was one.

CHAPTER TEN

WHITE BROTHER TO THE INDIANS

After two more days of travel, they arrived at Rabbit Portage. Its full name was Wapoose-ka-neemeech, or in English, The Place of Dancing Rabbits. It had been so named because rabbits were very thick at this place some years, and these animals have a way of thumping their hind feet rapidly on the ground, and by moonlight, when there are a number of them doing this, it appears and sounds very much as if they were dancing.

Shapian pitched their camp in a little bay near the post, where Chilawee could swim in safety, as the regular Indian camping-ground, though empty just now, would be swarming with hungry sleigh-dogs that had to find their living as best they could in the summer time, and would kill anything that was small enough, and eat anything that was not made of wood or iron; even very young children had to be kept out of their way. After the tent was up, and a good thick, springy floor of brushwood laid down, and wood had been collected and everything comfortably stowed in its place, Shapian took the canoe and went to visit the fur-post.

Here he found the trader, the same who had been to their home on that fateful day, earlier in the summer. He was new to the country, and could talk only a little Indian, and Shapian's English was not any too good. So the trader took him into his little private office behind the store, where they would not be interrupted, and here they managed somehow to understand one another. Shapian, standing before him upright as an arrow, explained matters as best he could. He told how everything had seemed to go wrong since Chikanee had been sold, and how his sister was all the time downhearted, and how lonely was Chilawee, and how unhappy they all were. And the trader, sitting there behind his desk, looking more like a judge than a trader, listened very closely to all that Shapian said, and when he had finished the white man said: "So Chila – who? –"

"Chilawee," corrected Shapian.

"Oh, yes," continued the trader, looking very severe. "So Chikalee, he's eh? And your sister too; and you want Chik – what's his name again – Chinawee back, eh?"

"Yes," answered Shapian patiently, "want Chikanee back."

And the trader cleared his throat rather gruffly, and gave a little snort. What nonsense, he thought, so much fuss over a little whining beast no bigger than a puppy.

But Shapian kept on in a low, even voice, picking his words slowly and carefully in the trader's language, of which he knew so little: "Me, I will work. I will make wood" (he meant "cut wood") "for your winter. I work all summer for you; also I sell you my gun. So I trade now, the wood and my gun for Chikanee. Those are my words, me." But they were words that trembled a little at the last, for his gun was very dear to him.

"I don't want your gun," said the trader sharply. "This post sold it to you, and we most certainly won't buy it back." And his hard blue eyes looked very fierce indeed.

Poor Shapian looked down at his moccasins to hide the trembling of his lips, and then proudly raised his head again, and said in his low voice: "Then I work all winter as well, me: all one year I work for you. One year for Chikanee."

Fiddlesticks, thought the trader. Was the boy crazy? It was plain to be seen that he knew very little about Indians. Suddenly he asked: "Did you see the fire?"

"Yes," replied Shapian. "Me, Sajo, Chilawee, pass through fire; one portage burning up. Pretty near finish,

79

us."

The white man stared hard at him – through the fire! "Preposterous!" he was about to say, but he thought better of it, and made only another gruff sound in his throat. For even he could not help seeing how much in earnest the Indian boy was; and then, seeing this, he was really sorry, for he knew that he could do nothing. Chikanee had been sold again, this time to some city people who had a park where wild beasts were kept in cages (Chikanee a wild beast!), and a live beaver was a rare and valuable animal. He explained all this to Shapian, still speaking roughly ("masterfully" as he put it) because he was new to trading and thought that it was the right way to speak to Indians – though he was not quite the ogre he made himself out to be, and he finished by feeling the least bit uncomfortable. And he talked in as kindly a tone as he was able to, when he told Shapian that Chikanee (Chikaroo this time!) had been gone a month now, and had been sold for fifty dollars.

Fifty dollars! Shapian's heart sank – fifty dollars, he had never seen such a sum. Traders hardly ever gave money; they gave goods in exchange for fur, because the Indians would only have to spend the money in the same store they got it from in the first place, at the post, so it was hardly worth the trouble of carrying around. Fifty dollars – his offer of work, and his precious gun, both refused! And he had nothing else to give. But it was not his way to give up quickly, and he went back to camp and told Sajo that he had found out just where Chikanee was. And she was very glad at this piece of news; for he never told her how hard-hearted the trader had been, nor about the large sum of money that they would never be able to get. So Sajo thought that there was nothing to do now but wait until Shapian had cut a little wood, and earned their fare to the city and back (it couldn't be very much, people came and went every few days!), and a little besides to buy back Chikanee with. And, in a way, she was right; that was all there was to do. But she didn't know how hopeless it all really was.

So Shapian bore his load of misery alone, and racked his brains to think of a way to earn fifty dollars; and as for the railway fare he had been afraid to even ask about it. All night he tossed and turned in his blanket while he planned and planned. If only they could just get to the city somehow. He had heard that some of these white people were kind, especially the city people; not all like the traders. If he could get down there and tell the folks who owned Chikanee how things were and how miserable everybody was, perhaps they would let Chikanee go home with Sajo, while he stayed behind and worked for them till the little prisoner's freedom had been paid for. Otherwise, he was sure, the whole expense would come to a hundred dollars. Poor Shapian! He could think of no greater amount of money than a hundred dollars. He had heard spoken of as rich an Indian who had earned a hundred dollars real money; this man had been out as a forest guide with a party of Americans. These Gitchie Mokoman – Big Knives, as the Indians called the Americans – were not hard to work for; they expected their guides to be friends, not servants, so the men of the village said, and they paid very high wages and often gave away their tents, or blankets, or guns, even whole camping outfits, after the trip was over. And at that thought a new idea came to him; and it was this.

Every second or third day there came up river to Rabbit Portage a big, clumsy-looking paddle-steamer, a wood-burner with two decks and huge wheels on its sides, in boxes. This unlikely-looking craft made the journey back and forth to the railway, and numbers of Americans came up on it from time to time. It was quite likely that some of them would need a guide, he considered, and this was work that he was well able to do. Full of this fresh plan, he hurried over to the post as soon as he had had his breakfast; but there was no one there except the trader until nearly noon, when the steamer was expected. Shortly before mid-day this cumbersome vessel chugged its way up the river and came in to the dock in a grand sweeping half-circle and with a great shouting of orders, and bell-ringing, and all the fuss and bustle to be expected of the one and only real, live steamboat in the entire country.

Sure enough, a crowd of tourists came ashore with their camping outfits, each having enough, to Shapian's notion, to supply at least forty people. They looked curiously at the Indian boy, with his buckskin moccasins and long braided hair, the first real Indian that some of them had ever seen, and one or two pointed black boxes towards him and clicked them at him. Shapian was ashamed and shy in front of all these people, who were so noisy, who dressed so strangely, and whose faces were either so very red or very pale. And suddenly he felt very small and very much alone before them all, and he knew that never could he be brave enough to guide even one of them. He turned to walk away as fast as he possibly could, without actually running, when he heard a voice calling out in Indian:

"Wait, my son, wait: I want to speak with you."

He had seen no Indians there, but he stopped, and looking back, saw coming towards him someone who was speaking in the Ojibway language quite as well as he did himself, yet who was not an Indian at all, but a white man, tall and strong-looking, with bright yellow hair and blue eyes – not hard blue eyes like the post manager had, but smiling, kind blue eyes. His white shirt was open at the throat, and his sleeves were rolled up above his elbows; all of his skin that showed was tanned by the sun, almost to the same colour as an Indian's. And he wore moccasins; though Shapian noticed that he walked a little carefully in them, as though he was not very well used to them. And the stranger came close to him and put his hand on the boy's shoulder, and asked if he was the son of Gitchie Meegwon. Shapian in reply nodded, and somehow he was no more shy or awkward, and saw only the smiling brown face, and heard only the words of this fair-haired man who spoke his language so well, using all the soft tones that Shapian was accustomed to.

"Do not be afraid," said the yellow-haired man (Shapian had already named him Yellow Hair, in his own mind). "These are all good people, Gitchie Mokoman – Americans. They like Indians, and only want to take your picture." Just the same, he drew Shapian away, as he went on: "But let us go to your camp and talk. I want to hear about your adventures in the fire, and besides, I have wished to see the children of Gitchie Meegwon this long time." He said that he knew Big Feather very well, calling him Quill, as all the white people did.

And Shapian felt right away that this was a friend, and his heart warmed towards the man, and although he had known him only so short a time, he felt that here, at last, was someone he could trust. And so he led his new friend through the woods to the camp, not taking him in the canoe, as he had always heard that a white man would upset you in so small a canoe – though he afterwards found out that this brown young man could handle a canoe very well indeed.

Sajo had been getting dinner ready, but when she saw them coming she ran and hid herself in the tent, for, besides the trader, whom she hated, she had never seen a white man so close before. But when she heard the visitor talking Indian so well, and heard his laugh, she peeped out, and found herself looking fair and square into the kindest pair of eyes that, next to her father's, she had ever seen – and then she knew she was caught, and so came out, and sat by the fire and pretended to be extremely busy with the pots and dishes. Just the same, she wanted very much to look at this stranger, and so she pulled her head-shawl well over her face, and peeked out at him from under it. And every so often he would catch her at it, and she would blush and bob her head down, so the shawl hid her face again, and would get so busy around the fire that at last there really was some cooking done. And so they all had dinner together. And Shapian felt for him even more respect, when he found that this white man could seat himself on the ground as comfortably as any Indian – something that he had so far never seen any white man able to do, except the trappers, who are often, themselves, very like Indians in their ways.

And the yellow-haired man praised the cooking and said he had not enjoyed such a meal for a long time; although it had been only bannock, with lard instead of butter, and some strips of dried deer meat, and tea without any sugar. But from the way he acted, you would never have known that it was not a feast.

After dinner their guest lit a cigarette and smoked awhile. Sajo found this to be a very strange way of smoking. All the Indians, including a good many of the women, used pipes, but she had never seen a cigarette before. And while he smoked he told them about himself. He was a Missionary, not – he put in hastily – one of the interfering kind that wanted to change *all* the Indian customs and beliefs, some of which though perhaps not all, he thought were very beautiful; nor did he want to force his own particular way upon them, but he was one who felt towards them as a brother. He had learned the Indian language from books, and moved from place to place amongst the Bush Crees, the Salteaux, the Algonquins and Ojibways (all of whom talk a similar language), working among them, teaching school, taking care of the sick, and trying to bring happiness wherever he could. And all because he felt that all the people of the world belonged to one great family, and believed that the Great Spirit loved and cared equally well for both red men and white, and he wanted to work for Him. And he told them how there were good people in the cities who paid all his expenses so that he was able to give his full time to this work, without having to ask the Indians for anything.

And this Indian boy and girl listened in wonder to hear such things, for they had always supposed that the Indians had been forgotten, and that no one cared any more about what happened to them, now that their land had been taken away from them. But they could not help but believe that this man was what he said, a brother to them, even though his skin did show to be so very white wherever the sun had not touched it, and though his eyes were not black like theirs, but blue as the sky itself at noon-day.

About this time Chilawee, who had been drying himself off after his latest bath and combing himself in the tent, hearing all the talking, and having, I suspect, more than an inkling that something was going on in the way of dinner, now came tumbling out to see what it was all about, and seeing the stranger, at once decided that he must be examined. On his way over he came to the dinner-table, which was nothing but a clean, white sheet of canvas laid upon the ground, with the dinner things still on it, and he walked right across this, tramping among the dishes, until he arrived in front of the visitor, and he then sat up on his hind legs and took a good close look at him. Perhaps he thought that such a large visitor ought to be good for quite a lot of bannock, if properly handled – anyhow, what he saw seemed to please him very much, for he began to shake his head back and forth, and from side to side and shook his body, quite in his old way of dancing, and presently fell on his back among the dishes, where he continued to squirm and wiggle. And there was a magnificent clatter, and a great upsetting, and spilling, and a scatteration of cups and plates, so, to quieten things down, Sajo hurriedly gave him a big chunk of bannock, expecting him to go back in the tent to eat it. But he was not to be so easily bribed to leave the company, and he squatted right there on the table-cloth, and taking his bannock in both hands, commenced to thoroughly enjoy himself – keeping one bright black eye on the visitor.

And this was the first time that he had ever done his funny dance since Chikanee had gone away; so that Sajo took if for a sign, and was more sure than ever that things were going to work out for the best. Yellow Hair, for his part, thought this performance was about the funniest thing he had ever seen.

Then Yellow Hair asked them how they came to have a beaver, which is the shyest of all animals, so tame, though he already knew most of their story from the trader; and he asked them many more questions. And although they were not, at first, very willing to tell him, he at last (he was very clever at questions, was this young man), heard how the two little beavers had been saved, and how they had been a birthday gift to Sajo from her father, and how they came to be named Chilawee and Chikanee – Big Small and Little Small. And how sad they all had been since Little Small had been taken away from them, and how unhappy and lonely poor Chilawee had become, and he listened (he was a very good listener too) while they told how they had started out to search for their little friend, and on the way had nearly lost their lives in the forest fire. And Shapian, at the end, said that he must now find work so as to have money to go to the city and bring Chikanee home again.

And after he had heard it all, the young man looked grave, and became very quiet, and the laughter was quite gone from off his face; for he knew that there was no work for Shapian, though he kept it to himself. And he reached out thoughtfully and stroked the soft, silky fur of the little

86

beaver and said, half to himself, in English: "So this is Big Small; and Little Small is far away, alone in the city. And these children – this must not be!"

And he stole a glance at Sajo, for he had noticed her pull her shawl, which had fallen across her shoulders, back over her head again; and he could see beneath it two big tears rolling slowly down her cheeks, though she had tried very hard to keep them back.

So he arose then, and went away. But before he left he said to them: "I am your friend, and your father's friend. Tomorrow I will return, and we will have dinner together again. Perhaps I can take away this cloud that lies so dark across your trail. I do not know, but I will try very hard.

And with a wave of his hand he was gone.

CHAPTER ELEVEN

THE BIG KNIVES

Immediately after his return to the post, the Missionary had a long talk with the trader in his office. Soon he came out with a sheet of paper marked "NOTICE," which he tacked on the door of the building. The tourists were still around at that time of the day, and several of them saw him doing this, and right away they all had to see what was on the notice. It called everyone to a meeting that was to be held, at four o'clock, in the Indian school-house on the hill behind the store, on a matter of great importance. In so small a place the news quickly spread, and, having nothing better to do, and rather wondering what this busy-looking fellow might have to say, everybody that could go, went.

The room was small, and some had to stand outside, listening in at the windows and the door. The young man with the yellow hair stood upon the teacher's platform, and when everyone was settled he began to speak. At first you could hear a little whispering, and coughing, and shuffling of feet, but this soon died down as he went on, and pretty soon everybody was listening, listening very hard. For he was telling the people a tale; something very different from what they had expected, something such as they had never heard before. He was as good at tales as he was at questions, this White Brother to the Indians. And the tale he told them was the story of Sajo and Shapian, of Big Small and Little Small.

And at the last he said: "– for we are still our brother's keeper. And let us remember that these young people who have braved the dangers of the Wilderness as perhaps you and I could not have done, whose colour is perhaps different from ours, whose language is not our language, and whose ways are not our ways, are *our* responsibility, yours and mine. They are not just a couple of Indian kids, but two very unhappy children. And who knows they may not be right in what they think, and that those small beasts that are their friends may have, after all, feelings that are very like our own.

"And let me say, before you go, that as you pass out through the door you will find, on the right, a large, empty Hudson's Bay tea-can! How about it, folks!"

When he had finished, the place broke out into a kind of a mild uproar, and everybody seemed to want to speak at once, and the ladies were saying "Oh! Did you ever hear –" and "Imagine, all that way alone!" and "– poor dears, through that dreadful fire!" And stood up and reached into their pockets, and talked loudly to one another, and made such remarks as, "Why, I wouldn't have missed this for anything," and "Where are they? We've go to do something about it." And one of them asked, "Where did he say the can was?"

And as the people began to file out through the door there came, from the direction of the tea-can, cheerful clinking sounds, and the crackle of crisp new bills and the rustle of old ones; and not all one-dollar bills either, but two's and five's, and the odd ten as well.

And last of all the trader went out also; and when he came to the door he looked carefully around to make sure that no one was looking, winked one eye (the one furthest from the tea-can), and reaching out quickly as though he were afraid of being seen, dropped into the can a tightly folded little wad of bills, and was heard to mutter to himself: "Well, Chikawee, or Chilakee, or Chikalee, or whatever you call yourself, here's good luck to you!"

But this White Brother, who was still on the platform, was not only good at questions and answers, and at telling stories; he also had remarkably good eyesight. And *he* saw.

Later in the day Yellow Hair went over to the children's camp, and when Shapian saw all that money he could hardly believe it was for him.

He was even a little frightened and asked: "What must I do – what work do they want me to do?"

"Nothing," answered Yellow Hair. "There is no time to work. You must go at once, or perhaps your little friend will be gone – animals get so lonely they sometimes die. These Gitchie Mokoman, they say I am to tell you that it is a gift. Long ago, the nation to which they belong was very cruel to the Indians, and they know now that wrong was done, and they are sorry; now they want to help. They are a great and generous people. All they ask is, that sometime, when you meet someone in trouble, help them if you can."

"Oh! I will, I will," said Shapian earnestly. "Tell them I will, and that I thank them." And the tears stood in his eyes, where all his troubles had never been able to bring them. And so the roll of money was placed carefully in an envelope, while Sajo looked on, her eyes big and round with joy and excitement; she knew nothing whatever about money, but now, she thought, there was nothing between them and Chikanee, nothing at all. She was glad, but not a bit surprised, and she said she had just *known* that everything was going to be all right, and that the white people were not *nearly* as bad as they were made out to be, and that it only went to show how true her dream had been!

In the envelope Yellow Hair enclosed a note to the station agent at the railway station, asking for two return tickets to the city. And although this looked like nearly all the money in the world to Shapian, after the railway fares were paid there would be very little left; for, although the tourists had been generous, there had not been, after all, very many of them. And the Missionary thought to himself that perhaps Shapian might have to stay behind and work out the price of Chikanee's liberty, if the park owners would consider such a thing. Anyhow, the only thing to do was to try. Yellow Hair also gave Shapian a letter addressed to the head man of the group of workers to which he belonged, who would find lodgings for them, and told him that as soon as he arrived in the city, he should ask to be taken to a policeman, and then show him the address on the envelope. The Missionary explained very carefully what a policeman looked like and how he would be dressed, and made Shapian practise saying the word – though the nearest he got to it was "poliss-man"; but this was considered to be quite plain enough to be understood. Chikanee, he told them, had been sold to the owner of an Amusement Park in the city, and any policeman could take them there.

And now, thought Shapian, with any luck at all, they should be back in time to welcome their father home, as the brigade was expected to return soon; and, he reflected, it was a lot easier to explain things when something you did, that was a little against the rules, turned out to be all to the good.

Their friend helped them to collect a bundle of poplar feed for Chilawee, besides the bannock that Sajo had made, and he promised to take care of their canoe and camping outfit until they returned. And when, on the following day, the boat was ready to leave, everybody in the whole place was on the dock to see them off. Some of the American ladies had fallen right in love with little Sajo, calling her Brown Eyes, and Little Moccasins, and one of them named her Madame Butterfly. And the men shook hands with Shapian all round, and called him a brave fellow, and said they were proud to know him. Even Chilawee came in for his share of the attention, though I don't believe he liked it very well, for he turned his back on folks in a manner that was decidedly impolite, and carried on with his own small affairs. The trader was there, looking around very severely, as if he heartily disapproved of the whole business; for he was determined that no one should ever know that he had put any money into this ridiculous affair.

At the very last, the Missionary (who had been standing apart from the crowd looking at the trader, and was smiling to himself about something or another) came to the gang-plank just as Sajo and Shapian walked aboard, and took the hand of each of them, and patted the little beaver on the nose, and said: "Good luck to you, children of Gitchie Meegwon. I will tell your father everything. May you be successful, and all four of you come safely home again. We will be waiting."

That very day, three canoes could be seen approaching the burnt portage on which Sajo, Shapian and Chilawee had had their desperate adventure. The canoes came onward at terrific speed. In them were Indians, stripped to the waist, their long hair tied out of the way in knots on top of their heads. Silent, grim-looking men they were, their naked shoulders glistening with the sweat of hard paddling. The brown bodies bent and swayed and paddles flashed in the sunlight as the canoes drove down swiftly upon the portage. The first one had no more than touched land, when a man leaped ashore. It was Big Feather. The brigade had returned and Big Feather had found his cabin empty!

Throwing himself on his knees beside the water, he scraped away the litter of the fire, now cold, and found there the sharp V made by the bow of a canoe; and he saw too, a small moccasin track, half washed away. Springing to his feet, he shouted: "They have passed here. Quickly! Take axes, clean out the portage, I will search the trail for —"

He stopped as an old man with white hair and a wise,

wrinkled face, said: "Stay, my son. My old eyes have seen many things. Stay and rest yourself. *I* will first cross the trail; perhaps I may read –"

And Gitchie Meegwon bowed his head to the words of his Chief, and waited, patiently. The trail was piled high with blackened, twisted trees, criss-crossed in every direction. The men chopped furiously among the fallen timber to open a passage for the canoes, while Gitchie Meegwon, unable to rest, busied himself cooking for the others, for the work would take no little time.

The old man went on across the portage, and searched very carefully among the wreckage of the fire, for whatever there might be of tracks or other traces of the children. He lifted aside any logs that lay flat on the ground that he was able to move, and looked beneath them very closely for tracks or signs of any kind. For fire sometimes moves so quickly that it leaves its work half done in places; and under one of these fallen logs, crushed but only partly burnt, he found the top of Chilawee's basket. He found, too, at the far end, a deep cut in the soft soil of the landing, where a canoe must have been driven very violently ashore – why, he asked himself, when it was going the other way? And then, looking out shrewdly at the huge tree, half burnt, that lay in the water no more than the length of two canoes away, he read the story to himself. For he was a very wise old man, and had been a warrior once, in days gone by, and could read the Wilderness as we read a book.

So he returned across the portage and told Gitchie Meegwon that he need sorrow no more. And he stood among the assembled Indians, with his flowing white hair and dark, strong face, and told them what he had found, and that he was sure that the children had escaped the Red Enemy. And Gitchie Meegwon, holding in his hands the scorched and blackened top of the basket, only wished he knew.

That night, after camp had been made and it had fallen dark, Big Feather climbed a great, bare, rocky hill that stood high above the face of the Wilderness, and there, with the wrecked and ruined forest stretching out on every side below him, his face painted in dark lines of sorrow, he raised his arms towards the sky and prayed aloud to the Great Spirit of the Wild Lands: "O-way! O-way! Manitou, Oh Spirit that watches over all the Forest People, keep my little ones from harm. Keep my children safe.

"Since they have gone my days lie dead around my feet, as do the ashes of this burnt and broken Wilderness.

"The Sun does not shine any more, and I cannot hear the Singing Birds. I hear only the laughing voice of Sajo; all I see is the face of my Shapian with his brave eyes, facing the flaming forest.

"Manitou, I have done wrong. The fault is mine, I, who brought sorrow to the heart of Sajo.

"Oh Gitchie Manitou, bring them safely back to O-pee-pee-soway, The Place of Talking Waters. Great Spirit of our people, keep my children safe.

"O-way-soam! O-way!"

And while his voice rang out across the empty, silent, burnt lands, there sat behind him in the moonlight the old white-haired Chief, with his wrinkled face and his eyes so full of wisdom, who tapped slowly, and softly, on a painted drum.

Meanwhile Sajo and Shapian, all unknown to their anxious father, were hastening farther and farther away from The Place of Talking Waters, speeding onwards through the darkness towards the distant city, as fast as the hurrying wheels of a train could take them.

CHAPTER TWELVE

THE LITTLE PRISONER

And meanwhile what of Chikanee? On the day the trader walked out of Gitchie Meegwon's camp with him, it seemed that Chikanee had left his friends for ever.

During the four or five days it took the trader, with his Ojibway canoe-men, to make the journey back to Rabbit Portage, Chikanee did not fare so badly, as one of the Indians took good care of him, keeping him well supplied with food and water. But he could not understand why Chilawee was not with him, and wondered where Sajo and Shapian had disappeared to. And he began to cry out for Sajo to come to him, as she had always done when she heard the little beaver calling. But no one came except the stranger Indian, and then only to change his water and to give him food. This man, by the trader's orders, accompanied Chikanee on the steamboat to see that he arrived safely at the railroad, and there left him; the money for him was paid over to the Indian, and what happened to him now did not greatly matter.

Having now come to a stop, and thinking that he must be home again, he wailed loudly for liberty and recognition, expecting Sajo to come and take him out of this stuffy and uncomfortable box. But no one came. So he started to chew at the box, and strange, harsh voices spoke angrily to him. He next tried to climb the walls of his prison, but they were too high, and these strangers shouted at him, and pounded on the box to keep him quiet, and now, thoroughly frightened, he lay still, whimpering and lonely. Where, oh where was Sajo, who had always comforted him in his small troubles, and in whose arms he had so often found such happiness? Where

95

was Chilawee, from whom he had never before been separated for so much as an hour?

A little later he was loaded on to a train that thundered and roared its way for many hours. When the train first started, forgetting as he did to close his ears, the noise drove him nearly crazy, and in his terror he tried to dive to freedom through his tiny dish of water, and upset it; so that besides his other misery he soon began to suffer from thirst. He had been snatched away from home too hurriedly for Sajo to have time to drop a bannock in the box, which would have lasted him several days, and no one now thought of providing him with anything to eat. And so sick, hungry, and wild with fear, he started desperately to cut his way out of the crate. In this he would have quickly succeeded, but striking a nail he broke one of his four cutting teeth, which made gnawing too painful to continue. His bedding, what little there was of it, became dirty, and the motion of the train thumped and bumped him against the hard sides of the box, so that he became bruised and sore. He tried hard to stay in the centre, away from the walls of his prison, but never could. One of the trainmen, intending to be kind, threw to him some crusts of bread from his own lunch but he thought that the little beaver's frantic clutchings at his hands was a sign of ill-temper (he was just a wild animal to these people, who did not know that he only wanted to be helped), and from then on they were afraid of him – so small a little creature to be afraid of! – and no one attempted to give him any more bedding or food, and his water-dish remained empty for the same reason.

And he raised his voice in cries of misery and called and called for his companions, who now could never hear him, wailed in his child-like voice for them to come and take away this great trouble that had befallen him. But no one paid any attention, if they ever even heard him, drowned as was his feeble outcry by the roar of the train.

At length, after many stops and starts, each of which jolted and slammed him from one hard side of his prison to the other, and a last, and cruelly rough ride in a delivery van, there came a sudden quietness. The cleats were taken from across the top of the box with a frightful screeching as the nails were drawn, and he was lifted out by a hand that held him very firmly by the tail; a large, strong hand, yet somehow a very gentle one. Then the other hand came up and was held against his chest as he hung head down, bringing him right end up, and a finger rubbed gently on one hot, tired little paw, and a deep voice spoke soothing words; so that suddenly he felt rather comfortable. For this man was a keeper of animals, and attendant in the park where Chikanee was to stay, and he knew his business very well. And when he examined his small captive, and saw how miserable, and bedraggled, and covered with dirt the little creature was – he who had been so proud and careful of his coat! – the keeper said angrily to the delivery man (who, poor fellow, was not to blame at all): "No water, nothing to eat, dry feet, dry tail, dry nose, teeth all broken up; if that isn't a shame, nothing ever was. Some way to ship a beaver, I'll say! But we'll soon fix you up, old-timer." For the man had been expecting his little guest, having had a letter about him, and had everything ready to receive him. Soon Chikanee found himself in an enclosure built of something like stone, but not nearly as friendly as stone, and surrounded by a rail of iron bars. And in this gaol of iron and concrete Chikanee, for no crime at all, was to spend the rest of his days.

Chikanee, gentle, lovable Chikanee, was now supposed to be a wild and probably dangerous beast!

It was not a very large place, a mere hutch after the freedom of the big lake beside which he had spent most of his short life, but that did not matter for the moment – he smelled water! And then he saw, right in front of him, a deep, clear pool; not a very big one, to be sure, but at least it was water. Into this he immediately threw himself and drank thirstily, floating on the surface, while the cracked and dried-out tail and feet soaked up the, to him, life-giving moisture, and the cakes of dirt loosened and washed from off him as he swam slowly back and forth. This seemed like the beaver's heaven itself, after more than three days of noise, starvation, dirt, and utter misery, and the hot, fevered little body cooled off and all the bumps and bruises ceased to throb, as the cool water slowly got in its good work on him.

And now, he thought, this must be just the plunge-hole. Down there, somewhere, lay the entrance, and through this he would set out and would, no doubt, come to his home-lake. Then Chilawee would run to welcome him and roll on his woolly back with joy, and Sajo would come and pick up, and hug him and make much of him, and whisper in his ear, and tickle him in that funny place under his chin, and all these times would be forgotten.

So, with a great splurge he dived straight down – to strike his head on the hard bottom of the pool, almost stunning himself. Again he tried, with the same result. He scratched and bit at the concrete, thinking to tear his way through it to the tunnel that must, somewhere, lead out of it. But he only cracked and split his claws and took more chips out of his remaining teeth. Then he scrambled out of the pool and over to the bars, and tried to squeeze through them; but they were too close together. He tried to gnaw at them, but his broken teeth never even scratched them. So he ran round and round inside the enclosure, stopping here and there to dig, but to no purpose. For a long time he worked, running back to the pool and out again to the bars, trying to gnaw, trying to dig; but it was useless. And then at last he realized that there was no opening anywhere, no plunge-hole, no escape; and weary, wretched and hopeless, he lay flat on the hard, hot floor of the pen and moaned, moaned as he had done when Sajo had nursed him to sleep - only then he had moaned with joy, and now it was from misery. And his paws ached for just one touch of Chilawee's soft, silky fur. And now there was no Sajo, no Chilawee, only one unhappy Little Small in prison, all alone.

The attendant stood by for a long time, and watched and shook his head, and said: "Too bad, little fellow, too bad." This was his job, taming these wild creatures that were sent to him from time to time; yet, liking animals as he did, he sometimes hated the work. To him they often seemed to be, not wild things at all, but hopeless, unfortunate little people who could not speak, and who sometimes were so pitifully in need of the kindness for which they could not ask; and he had always felt that a man, who was so much bigger and stronger, and knew so many things that they did not, should be good to them and help them all he could. And he pitied the little beaver that was struggling so helplessly to be free, for this was not the first one that had come under his care, and he knew their gentle nature. And stepping in through the gate of the pen, he picked up Chikanee carefully and cleverly, so that, as in the first place, he was not scared or excited, but was actually comfortable in his hands – they were so much more friendly than the concrete!

The keeper carried Chikanee to his cottage, which was close by, inside the park. He had three young children, and when they saw their father bringing in a little beaver, they crowded round to see, and they shouted with delight, so that Chikanee was afraid again, and tried to burrow into the man's coat; for already he had begun to trust him. And their father quieted his children and set the little creature on the floor, where, finding himself once more in a house, he felt a little more at home than in the cage.

They all stood watching to see what he would do, and the keeper's wife said: "The wee mite! Look how thin he is – Joey," to one of the youngsters, "go get an apple; those

99

other beaver we used to have were just crazy for apples."

So this Joey fellow went and got one right away, and put it down on the floor in front of Chikanee. He had never seen an apple before, but he sniffed at it, and Oh! what a wonderful smell came from it! And so he cut into it as best he could with his poor wee broken teeth and then, what a taste – the most delicious taste in all the world! And seizing hold of this wonderful tit-bit with both hands, he demolished nearly the half of it. At this the keeper was very pleased, for some of his prisoners refused all food, and died, but now he had seen him eat he knew that this one would recover. The children laughed to see him sitting up there like a little man while he ate, and the keeper's wife exclaimed: "There, didn't I tell you? He'll be all right in no time."

Then the keeper brought in the sprays of fresh, juicy poplar leaves he had placed in the pen for him, but which he had not touched. But now he ate them, and the children wondered to see him holding the leaves in little bunches in his hands while he put them in his mouth. Feeling a good deal better by now, he made small sounds of pleasure while he ate, and at that the young ones marvelled even more, and one, a little girl with golden hair and a round, rosy face, said:

"Listen, listen to him talk, just like a little, wee baby. Oh daddy, do let's keep him in the kitchen!" Their mother spoke up too: "Yes, Alec, let's keep him here for a spell; there's no one in the park – it's almost like putting a child in prison."

And Alec answered: "Perhaps you're right. We'll fix him a place in here for tonight."

So they made a place for our Chikanee in the kitchen, and Alec the keeper fastened a low, wide pan of water to the floor, and set a large box down on its side, with plenty of clean straw in it for a bed for him. And there the little beaver spent the night, not happily perhaps, but very comfortably.

The next morning Alec returned him to the pen, so that any of the public who came to the park could see him; but when evening came round again and the grounds were empty, the keeper brought him back to the cottage. And from then on he did this every day, and Chikanee spent all the hours when he was not "working" in the keeper's house, and in the kitchen had his bed, and his big pan of water, and ate his leaves and twigs there. And each day he had a nice, juicy apple, which quite made up for a lot of his troubles, though not for all of them; for never would he be anything but lonely so long as he lived. Every morning there was a considerable mess of peeled sticks, and cut branches, and left-over leaves, and the floor was all slopped with water, but the children willingly turned to and cleaned up, after Chikanee was carried away to his daily task of being stared at in the cage. Nobody seemed to mind the little trouble he was. He got along famously with the family and, in his own small way, soon became quite a part of the household.

As time went on he got to know them all, and he would romp clumsily with the youngsters; and to them he was a kind of tumbling, good-natured toy, like one of those stuffed toys to be found on Christmas trees. But to Chikanee, it could never be the same as it had been at O-pee-pee-soway, and often he didn't want to play, but lay quietly in his box, his little heart filled with a great empty longing for his old family.

Before very long his teeth had grown in, and he spent a lot of time sharpening them against one another, grinding and rattling them together at a great rate. His coat, which he had sadly neglected for a time, so that it had become all tangled and matted, now got its daily scrubbing and combing, and his small frame, that had for a while been little more than a bag of bones, soon filled out, and he began to look like the old Chikanee again. And in a way

101

he was happy; but never quite.

While in the cage he was really miserable, and the keeper knew this, and always felt badly when he put the little fellow in there each morning, and looked back at this pitiful little creature that gazed after him so wistfully as he walked away, sitting there alone on the bare cement floor, surrounded by bars that would have held a grizzly bear. He remembered that a beaver may live more than twenty years – twenty years in that prison of iron and concrete! In twenty years his own family would be grown up and away from there; he himself might be gone. The town would have become a great city (it was not really a very big place); people would come and go – free people, happy people – and through it all, this unhappy little beast, who had done no harm to anyone, and seemed only to want someone to be kind to him, would, for twenty long and lonely years, look out through the bars of that wretched pen as though he had been some violent criminal; waiting for the freedom that would never be his, waiting only to die at last. And, thought the keeper, for no good reason at all, except that a few thoughtless people, who never really cared if they ever saw a beaver, might stare for a minute or two at the little prisoner, and then go away and forget they had ever seen him. Somehow it did not seem fair, to this kind-hearted man, and when he watched the little creature rollicking with the children in his funny, clumsy way, he wished very much that there was something that he could do about it, and decided to give his small prisoner the freedom of the cottage as long as it was at all possible.

But Chikanee had not quite given up; he had one hope that for a long time he never lost. He quite expected that, in some mysterious way, Chilawee would come to join him; for in the old days, no matter where he had happened to be, it had not been long before Chilawee had turned up, looking for him. And so, every so often he searched for him very carefully, looking in the wooden hut that stood in the enclosure, going patiently all through the downstairs rooms of the cottage, and would sometimes take a run outside and examine the wood-shed very thoroughly, and was very sure that some day he would find him. But after a whole month of daily disappointments he began to lose courage, and at last gave up his search that always turned out to be such a failure.

And hundreds of miles away, Chilawee was doing the very same thing, and all for nothing.

Chikanee was just beginning to get over this when something took place that was very worst of all – and yet something that was very near to his dearest wish. One day an Indian woman, with a bright shawl on her head, passed by the pen. The moment he saw her, Chikanee dashed wildly at the bars, and reached through them with clutching paws, and he let out a piercing cry, for fear she would pass him by; at which the woman stopped and spoke to him, and the sounds she made were the same as he had heard so often in the Indian country, at home! But not the voice. And seeing her face, and catching the scent of her, he turned and plodded slowly back to the bare wooden hut again, more dejected and downcast than he had ever been.

He had thought it was Sajo.

But this experience stirred him, and brought new hopes to him; he got the idea that some day Sajo *would* come. And from then on he watched for her. Crowds of people visited the park in the afternoons, and most of them paused by his cage to see what a beaver was like. But his "customers" never stayed long, and soon passed on; to most of them he looked to be just a scrubby little pup with a flat tail. Some just gazed carelessly, others curiously, a few poked sticks at him and made harsh and, as he thought, threatening sounds; a few, a very few, pitied him, and one or two were friendly and gave him peanuts and candy – but none of them was Sajo. But he continued to hope, and spent his time watching closely every face he saw, sniffing every hand he could get near to. But he never saw the face he looked for, never caught the scent of that so-loved small hand. Yet he was sure that some day a well-remembered voice would call out "Chik-a-*nee*!, that the brown hands whose touch had so often thrilled his little body, would again pick him up, and then – Oh! the joy of once more pushing his nose close into that special spot in a certain warm, soft neck, there to puff and blow a little while and then to slumber, and forget!

Hours at a time he spent this way, watching, waiting, hoping; and later, in the cottage kitchen, he would think, in some dim and misty way, of the happy days that seemed now to have been oh, so long ago, and thought of the little house under Shapian's bed, that Chilawee and he had between them for their very own, and of the crazy, tiny beaver house, and all the other arrangements at which they had worked so bravely together. And at last he became listless, and kept to himself, even in the cottage; and he never played with the children any more. He neglected his coat, so that it became matted and unkempt. And he began to refuse his food, and would sit with his apple untouched in his hands, his head dropping, eyes closed, breathing fast and heavily.

And the keeper, looking at him sorrowfully, knew that there was no longer any need to worry about the twenty years; or any years.

Chikanee wasn't going to live.

And the tiny brain grew hot and feverish with longing, and he seemed sometimes almost to see his old friends there before him, and thinking of them fell asleep, and sleeping dreamed of them. For animals *do* dream, as perhaps you know, and often wake up half scared to pieces from a nightmare, the same as you or I, and from the sounds they sometimes make, some of their dreams must be quite pleasant too.

One evening he awoke from a dream of them that was so real that he thought himself once more at home with them, and he got up and ran whimpering about the kitchen, looking for them, and not finding them, cried out again and again in loud sobbing wails. And as he cried, his voice was like the voice of a small lost child.

For he did not, could not know, that less than one mile away, in another and similar room, was another similar little beaver, and that there with him, waiting for morning, too excited to even think of sleeping, were two little Indians – a boy that stood straight and proudly, like an arrow, and a little girl who had on a brightly coloured head-shawl.

And in one corner of the room there stood an old familiar, well-worn, birch-bark basket.

Yes, you guessed it. Sajo and Shapian had really come, at last.

CHAPTER THIRTEEN

PATRICK THE POLICEMAN

When the train on which Sajo, Shapian, and their small fellow-traveller Chilawee, were riding, made the last of its many stops and came to a standstill in the city station, the children were almost too scared to get off. The guard, who had kept his eye on them all the way, helped them out, spoke a few words of encouragement, and left them to attend to his other duties.

They found themselves in a world of noise. The hurrying throngs of people, the hiss of escaping steam, the clang of engine bells, the shriek of whistles and the thunderous bellowing of the mighty engines deafened and terrified them. Before, behind, and on every side of them was a terrific confusion and a ceaseless din. To them the station was a vast, echoing cave filled with terrifying sights and sounds, and never before had they felt so small and defenceless. They felt more alone here, in the midst of all these people, than they had ever done in the forest, with its silence and its quiet, peaceful trees. People looked at them curiously, but everyone seemed to be too busy rushing this way and that to pay much attention to them.

So there they stood, in all that deafening uproar, two young people from the Silent Places, as scared and bewildered, and nearly as helpless, as the two tiny kitten beavers had been when Gitchie Meegwon found them floating on the Yellow Birch river. Yet Sajo, with all her fear, had only one thought – Chikanee had come through all this *alone*! While Shapian began to wish himself back in the forest fire again, among the friendly animals, Chilawee, for his part, closed his ears as tight as two tiny black purses and lay perfectly still, jammed tight into a corner of his basket.

They had been standing there for what seemed like an hour (though it had really been only a few moments), and Shapian was thinking of making *some* kind of move towards a huge door through which crowds of people were flowing like a swift, rushing river, when there stopped in front of them a young boy. He was about Shapian's own age, and was dressed in red, with bright buttons all down the front of his short, tightly fitted coat, and a little hat that looked more like a very small, round box than anything else. It was the kind of uniform worn by a page boy in a smart hotel.

"Hullo, you kids," he said cheerfully. "Are you lost? Who are you looking for?"

Poor Shapian, confronted by this self-possessed and magnificent-looking person, found that he had completely forgotten any English he ever knew, and could remember only one word; so he said it.

"Poliss-man," he stammered nervously.

"You want a policeman, eh?" said the page, who got to the point at once. "OK. Come along with me." And beckoning to them he set off at a great pace, his shiny boot-heels tapping sharply on the hard platform. The Indians, silent-footed in their moccasins, slipped softly along behind him, though they almost had to trot to keep up, Shapian carrying Chilawee's basket in one hand and holding tightly on to his sister with the other. It must have been a queer-looking procession. Their guide steered them through the crowds, over to the entrance and down a great hall filled with more people (nearly all the people in the world, thought Shapian), and brought them over to a big, stout man who stood beside a door at the far end. He also had a number of shiny buttons on his coat.

"Hey, Pat," the page called to him. "Here's a couple of kids want to see a policeman," and pushed them forward, continuing – rather disrespectfully, "You shouldn't be

107

hard to see, you're big enough. Look like Indians to me – better watch your scalp!" And with an impudent grin at the police officer and a wink at the children, he dodged into the crowd and disappeared.

"Oho," exclaimed the policeman loudly, looking down on the two youngsters, with his hands behind his back. "Oho, so it's scalps, is it?" said he, looking very fiercely at them, as though he were about to take them prisoner – though his eyes had an odd twinkle about them and were pleasantly crinkled at the corners. " 'Tis young Injuns, eh? Well, 'tis a mighty poor scalp you'll get from me, that's been bald as an egg this twenty years; and well did the little imp know it that brought you here!"

He was built something on the lines of Father Christmas, and although he talked so fiercely, his face was round and cheerful, and he wore his helmet a little to one side of his head in rather a jaunty sort of fashion, as though being a policeman was the most entertaining business imaginable. But seeing that the Indians were becoming alarmed, he asked, in what he considered to be a lower voice: "And what can I be doin' for you?"

"You – poliss-man?" asked Shapian timidly.

"Yes, me lad," answered the constable, putting his helmet just a trifle more to one side, "I'm a policeman, and a good one – the O'Reillys have ever been of the best – Hello! What's in the basket?" For Chilawee had now begun to wail.

"A-mik," answered Shapian, taking off the lid for him to see and repeated "A-mik," at which, to his great astonishment, the policeman began to laugh very loud indeed. "Ho-hoho-hoho! So it's a Mick he calls me; knew I was Irish right away to be sure – sharp as a di'mond! You said it, me boy, I'm a Mick, sure I'm a Mick." For he was very proud of being Irish, and imagined that Shapian had known it when he used the Indian word "A-mik," which means of course "Beaver." He thought this Indian lad

108

very smart to have discovered it; and Shapian, hearing him say so often that he was "a Mick," came to the conclusion that he belonged to some strange race of white men who called themselves "Beaver," a very honourable title indeed!

"And where would you be wantin' to go?" now asked the policeman.

At last Shapian remembered the letter Yellow Hair had given him, and pulling it out gave it to the officer. He read the address on the envelope and said: "I see. I'm on duty and cannot leave; but sit you down and wait, and I'll take you there. And it's Patrick O'Reilly himself will see that no harm comes to you." And he patted Sajo kindly on the head, and Shapian having at last been able to tell him in English what Chilawee really was, he asked to see him, and pronounced him to be a "fine little fellow, what there was of him," as he didn't see a great deal, for the bold Chilawee had become very meek indeed, and he hid his head, and his tail, and all his legs and feet and made himself as small, and, as he thought, as invisible as possible.

And so the two young wanderers, feeling a good deal more at their ease, sat on the end of a long row of seats and waited. And the big policeman, who seemed to be in such continual good humour over nothing at all, asked them a number of questions, and Shapian, having got his English into pretty fair working order by now, told him most of the story. And the listener became quite depressed about it, and said that he – Patrick O'Reilly himself, mind you – would take them to the people who owned the park. "And it's myself as will tell them the plain truth, with both hands, so I will," he said aloud.

A little later he was relieved by another constable, who joked good-naturedly with him about the "family" he had got for himself, and they then went out together on to the street, where there were less people, and there was not so much bustle and noise. Their new friend talked nearly the whole time, for he was doing his very best to make them feet at home, and Shapian talked too, in his queer, broken English. Sajo was all eyes and ears, though she could not understand anything; but she felt that they were safe with this big, blue-coated man beside them; and now no longer afraid, she felt like crying out with happiness, for was not Chikanee right here, in this very city, perhaps on this self-same street? And she began to enjoy looking around at the wonders that were to be seen on every side – horses, which she had heard about, but never seen before, the tram cars that sailed along so nicely without even a horse to draw them, ladies in beautiful clothes, and best of all, the bright shop windows. Once they passed a restaurant, and the smell of food, and the sight of the delicious-looking pies and cakes in the window, brought their weary little faces round so sharply in that direction, that the policeman, noticing it, and hearing them whisper together in Indian, guessed right away that they were hungry.

"Well, now," he exclaimed, "and it's hungry you are, and me blatherin' away like some old gossip. 'Tis not the way of the O'Reillys to leave a friend starvin' to death on the doorstep, so to speak. We'll go in and have a bite."

"Yessplease," said Shapian. "My sister, that's hungry long time now," though it would have been hard to say which of them was the hungrier. So Patrick herded them into the place ahead of him, and after they were seated he asked them when they had eaten last, and Shapian told him: "At trading post. Me, I have not that fear; but my sister, now have plenty. So sit down all time one place, eat nothing. Me, I take care my sister. That's never leave him alone, my sister. So nobody eat, only little bit Chilawee his bannock."

And the policeman said: "You're a brave lad. The O'Reillys, now –" But at this moment the waiter came in with their order, and the children's eyes grew round as door-knobs, and very nearly as big, when they saw the tray piled high with cheerfully steaming food. And it all looked so tantalizing, and smelled so delicious, that when the dishes were set before them they were quite over-powered, and Sajo even felt a little faint, so excited was she. Soon they were too well occupied either to talk, look, or listen, or do anything else but eat, and eat; and there was some wonderfully fast work done around that table in the next few minutes. And while they were so enjoying themselves, Sajo remembered that poor Chilawee must be hungry too, and she put tit-bits from off her plate into the basket, of bread and butter, and doughnuts, and pie, and soon he was as busy as the rest of them, making up for a whole lot of lost time.

When the feast was pretty well over and nobody, not even Chilawee, could possibly have eaten one more mouthful, everybody sat back and began to feel ex-ceedingly comfortable. The policeman lit a cigar, and being, if possible, in even better humour than before, beamed around on his guests in a state of the highest satisfaction. His helmet was off, and Shapian, being no longer busy, now had time to see that he was not quite so bald as he had claimed to be – bald as an egg, he had said – for a wide ring of hair started just above one of his ears and worked back, and around, till it come to the other ear.

Sajo, like the good little housekeeper she was, piled all the dishes neatly away to one side, finding it great fun to handle these rich-looking things. They were really nothing more than ordinary china table-ware; but Sajo had never *seen* such dishes, as she told Shapian that night.

It was warm in the small room, and Sajo put back her bright head-shawl, showing her long, shining black braids and her soft, dark eyes, all alight with happiness just now, and the officer, who saw her face properly for the first time, said she was the prettiest little girl he had ever seen since he'd left Ireland. And Shapian told her what he had said, and she blushed and hung her head, and pulled the head-shawl up again. But no one could be shy very long with this good-natured man, and she soon got over it and looked up at him, so that her shawl slipped back again, and this time she left it there, and she laughed at all the things he was saying, although she couldn't understand a word of it. And Shapian, glad to see his sister so light-hearted, laughed nearly as much as she. And officer O'Reilly, laughed so heartily that he was obliged to open his coat, and mop his bald spot with a large red handkerchief that he pulled out of his sleeve; and they were all in uncommonly high spirits. Even Chilawee made himself heard, and he and Sajo had a little private conversation of their own, while Patrick O'Reilly tried his hand at learning to talk Indian from Shapian. He didn't make very much progress; but there is one word that Indians use very often, "kaeget," which means "certainly," or "indeed," and if you are *very* sure, you say "Kae-*get*." Now, this was easy to say, and Patrick caught on to it very soon, and when Shapian told him what it meant, he practised it until he had it right, and from then on it was kae-*get* this, and kae-*get* that, and he was very proud of his new word. And so he explained the plans he had made for the next day, talking, as nearly as he could, in Shapian's broken English:

"That park," he said, following Shapian's own style, "that park, closed." Here he closed the door of the room, very firmly. "Tomorrow, open park, give money, beaver come!" And opening wide the door, threw out his arm like a "go-ahead" traffic signal and stood aside, as though he expected a whole troop of beaver to come marching in through the opening. Then he brought out the letter, and tapping it said: "Me, come this place. Tomorrow. You wait." And with another flourish of the signal, "Kay-*get*."

Shapian, whose English was not quite as bad as all that,

and found it hard to keep from smiling, understood very well, and said so; and the good Pat O'Reilly was very pleased with his first lesson in Indian, and really felt that he began to understand something of the language.

He saw his "family" safely to their address, and turned them and the letter over to the manager of the place, making sure they understood that he would be back for them in the morning, telling them on no account to move until he came. The manager seemed to be expecting them; in fact, he had already received a telegram about them, and as soon as he had shown them to their room, he sent a telegram himself. And at the same time, in his own modest home, the policeman was holding a long telephone conversation about them; also up at the distant fur-post Rabbit Portage, there was a considerable stir taking place on their account. And altogether, there was quite a fuss going on over these three wanderers – a fuss about which they knew nothing whatever.

Upstairs, the two children talked excitedly, but in whispers, for somehow this grand, white-walled room gave them a feeling of being very small and out of place, like two mice that had stolen into somebody's pantry, or into a church.

But it was a place where no accidents could ever happen, that was certain, so, in the safety of this room, Shapian took out their little wad of money from a deerskin pouch that hung from a string about his neck. He spread it out and smoothed each note very carefully on the table, while Sajo looked on. They tried to make out just how much there was, Sajo standing by with her finger on her lips and her head on one side, looking very wise, while Shapian frowned and wondered, and looked closely at each bill; but the figures didn't mean a thing to them, and they had to give it up. But anyway, there was plenty, they agreed, more money than they had ever seen before; and Shapian folded it all up again and put it back into its little bag, under his shirt.

For this was the price of Chikanee's freedom, and must never, for one single moment, be out of reach.

Meanwhile Chilawee, on the floor, was having the time of his life in a tin basin; he was having, at the same time, another feast, from a loaf of bread which the manager had kindly supplied, and what part of it he had not been able to eat, was slowly being transformed into a mushy, gooey, sticky mess, and you can be sure that the rug on which all this was taking place was in no way improved by the performance.

Not one of them could sleep. The little beaver because there were far too many interesting things to be found in corners, and the children because tomorrow was to be that great, that wonderful Day of Days, for which they had worked so hard and gone through so many dangers, and for which they had waited so long.

For, whatever misgivings Shapian may perhaps have had, Sajo, sure that her dream was coming true, never once doubted, and only said: "Tomorrow we have Chikanee. I *know*."

CHAPTER FOURTEEN

TOGETHER AGAIN

Early the following day, Patrick O'Reilly called for his charges, as he had promised. But they did not go right away to the animal park as they had expected, but to a large building in the city, where the owners had an office.

Afraid that at the last moment some accident might happen to the money, Shapian often felt at the lump under his shirt, where the little bag was; they were going to need it very soon now, and he was getting nervous. In the other hand he carried Chilawee in his basket, and beside him Sajo walked with short, little-girl steps, her shawl wrapped about her head and shoulders.

There was a swift ride in a lift, which they far from enjoyed, and then they found themselves, with the Irishman beside them, standing before a desk behind which sat a man. He was youngish with a pale, narrow face and a weak-looking chin, and a cigarette in the corner of his mouth was burnt down almost to his lips. He spoke without removing the cigarette, squinting sharply at them. "Well, what do you want?" he asked shortly.

Sajo, who up till now had had such faith in her dream, became suddenly fearful and anxious, and trembled like a leaf.

There was a moment's silence, a very heavy, thick kind of silence. Then: "Sir," said Patrick, "I telephoned Mr Hawkins last night concerning me young friends here, to talk over a small matter of business like –"

"You can do your business with me," broke in the young man, in no very friendly tone. "Mr Hawkins is busy at present." And he glanced towards a door that led into another room, which stood slightly open.

115

"You see, 'tis this way," began Patrick once more, when the young man looked at his wrist-watch and m busy interrupted again: "Make it snappy, constable; I'this morning."

Patrick got a little red in the face, and again started his speech, this time successfully. It was a speech that he had carefully rehearsed the night before, the story that, as he had said at the railroad station, was going to "bring tears to the eyes of a heart of stone." Evidently the young man did not have a heart of stone, however, for there were no tears; in fact, while the policeman was talking, he looked several times at his wrist-watch, and lit a fresh cigarette from the stump in his mouth. Far from having a heart of stone, it began to look very much as though he had no heart at all. Patrick became a little discouraged towards the last, and finished his tale rather lamely:

". . . so the young people wants to buy the little beast back from you: and I'll be so bold as to say that I think you'll be doin' the Lord's own work if you let them have it." And having done his best he stood there, nervously wiping his face with the big red handkerchief.

The man straightened some papers on the desk and leaned back in his chair. "Are you quite done?" he enquired coldly.

"Yes," answered Patrick, none too happily, for he began to fear, and with good reason, that he had lost the battle already.

"Oh," said the clerk, "thank you. Well, let me tell you" – his words fell like chips of ice on a plate of glass – "that beaver was bought in a fair and perfectly business-like way, and not from these ragamuffins at all, but from a reputable trader. We paid fifty dollars for him, which was a great deal more than the little brute was worth, and we have no intention of selling him back – unless we can get a good profit on the deal, and" – here he looked at the two little Indians – "I don't think your red-skinned *friends,*

116

as you call them, are very well off judging by their looks."

Patrick turned redder than ever, but shrewdly suspecting that money alone could talk to this hard-headed fellow, he pushed Shapian forward.

"Money," he whispered hoarsely, "that money. Money, give it now!" And Shapian, sick with fear, for he had understood nearly everything, stepped forward, fumbled for a moment in the pouch, and dropped his little wad of money on the desk.

The clerk took it, counted it. He sniffed: "There's only fourteen dollars here." He handed it back. "Nothing doing," he said, and to make sure that everybody understood he added, for good measure, "All washed up; no sale; no good; no! Get me?"

They got him; every one of them.

Nobody spoke, nobody moved; but to Shapian it was the end of the world – but no – was this true? And then the silence seemed suddenly to be choking him; the white face of the man behind the desk was getting bigger and bigger, was rushing towards him – the floor seemed to be going from under his feet – was he going to fall like a woman, faint, like a weak girl! He closed his eyes to shut out the sight of that pale, weak face with its one eye that leered at him so mockingly; he gritted his teeth, clenched his fists, and stiffened his young body upright in his old, proud way; and the dizzy feeling passed, leaving him cold and trembling. Meanwhile the policeman stood helplessly by in his dismay, mopping his bald head and mumbling huskily, "Oh, the shame it is! The pity of it! And it's me that's betrayed them that trusted in me!"

And Sajo? She had been watching every move with painful eagerness, her eyes flitting from face to face like two frightened birds in a cage; and she had seen. No one needed to tell her.

They had failed. In just two minutes they had failed.

She came softly over beside Shapian. "I know, my

117

brother," she said very quietly, in such a strange little voice that Shapian looked at her quickly, and put his arm about her, while she stood close, looking up at him, "I know now. He is not going to give us Chikanee. I was wrong – about my dream. We have come to the city not to get Chikanee, after all. I think – perhaps – it was – to bring Chilawee to him. That must be what my mother meant; so they could be together – so they won't be lonely any more. That must be it. So –"

And her voice fell to a whisper, and the little dark head drooped. "Tell this man – I – give him – Chilawee – too."

And she set Chilawee's basket upon the desk and stepped back, her face like a sheet of paper, her lips pale, and her eyes wide and dry, staring at the basket.

O'Reilly, cutting short his lament, stood aghast; *now* what was going on?

"What's this?" exclaimed the clerk, becoming angry. And Shapian told him:

" 'Nother beaver, Chilawee. His brother, that Chikanee, very lonely. You keep him Chilawee too; not be lonely then. Those are words of my sister. Me –" His voice stuck in his throat, and he couldn't say any more.

"Well, now," said the clerk, smiling for the first time, though the smile improved his features very little. "That's a horse of a different colour! We'll fix that up very quickly," and he reached for his pen –

"NO!" suddenly shouted O'Reilly in a terrific voice, so that everybody jumped, and the ink-bottles and paper-weights and the pens and the pencils all jumped, and even the pale young man jumped, and turned a shade paler and his cigarette jumped from his lips to the floor.

"No, you don't," he bellowed in a tremendous voice. "No son of an O'Reilly will stand by and see a couple of helpless kids bullyragged and put upon by likes o' you. You're a black-hearted scoundrel," he roared. "An' I'm an officer of the law, an' I'll arrest you for conspiracy, an'

118

fraud, an' misdemeanour, an' highway robbery, an' assault, an' –" Here he ran out of the more attractive-sounding crimes, and started round the desk towards the now badly scared young man, who was backing away as hastily as possible in the direction of the other room, while Sajo and Shapian stood by with eyes as big as saucers. Just what this rather violent son of the O'Reillys intended to do, never became known, for at that moment the other door opened, and the fleeing young man found his line of retreat cut off, as he stumbled backwards into yet another guest to the party, and a voice, a very quiet, low voice said, "Pardon me". Just inside the room a slim, grey-haired old gentleman stood peering over his spectacles at this astonishing scene.

He gave a slight cough, and said again, "Pardon me, if I appear to intrude," and then invited, very politely, "Won't you sit down?"

Pat still snorted angrily and glared at his intended prisoner, who was not at all sure if he *hadn't* committed some crime or another, so that his hands trembled a little as he fumbled with a new cigarette.

"Pray sit down, gentlemen," again invited the grey-haired man.

They sat down; somehow you felt that you must do as this mild-mannered old gentleman asked you. And he it was that owned the park; it was Mr Hawkins himself.

"Now, let us talk matters over," he suggested, looking from the policeman to the clerk, then to the children and back to the policeman again. "Now, constable, on the telephone last night I promised to hear these children's story, and to consider what should be done. I have heard everything – from the other room, far better than if I had been here; for then certain things *did* happen, that would not otherwise have done so. I had already learned from you how far they have come, and what hardships and dangers they have been through to try and regain their

119

pet. But I had to be careful; I had to know that it was not a to fraud, and as I cannot understand their language, I wanted see what they would do, before I could even consider the matter. Now I know the *whole* story, and I see that matters are going to be very difficult – for me.

"Everyone is listening, I hope?" he continued. "Yes?" It was plain to be seen that he was very well used to having people listen to him; and he peered at Shapian and Sajo in turn, and the children found his gaze rather piercing, quite different from his voice.

"Ah," he said, finding that everybody was waiting to hear more (although Sajo did not understand a word he said). "Very good. Now, I heard these Indian children offer to give up their other pet, so the two animals could be together, which proves to me their truthfulness. But, there is my side to be thought of. As George, here, says, it was a perfectly proper piece of business, and it cost me quite a sum of money. I cannot decide all at once. Moreover, it is not good for people, especially young people, for them to have everything they ask for – not, that is, unless they have worked for it." And he looked at them a trifle severely.

"And what are you going to do, Sir?" asked O'Reilly anxiously, wishing that he would stop talking and get down to business.

But Mr Hawkins turned to his clerk: "You are a good business man, George; almost too good, I sometimes think."

"I was only doing my duty, Sir," answered George, with some truth.

"Ah, our duty; yes," mused the thoughtful Mr Hawkins. "Well, no matter."

"But what are ye goin' to do about it, Sir?" again asked Pat, nearly exploding with impatience.

"Do?" queried this exasperating old man. "Do? Oh, yes; I think I have decided what to do – just this!" And taking Chilawee's basket he beckoned the children over. "There," he said gently, "there is your small friend. Now" – and becoming all at once very brisk and businesslike, he wrote something on a card and handed it to Patrick "and now, go down to the park with Mr O'Reilly, *and get the other one.* He is yours; you most certainly have earned him." Shapian stared, his mouth open – did he hear correctly? Or was this another one of Sajo's dreams in which he had become entangled? Or perhaps it was one of his own! But Sajo was very much awake, and she grabbed Chilawee's basket from him.

"Tell me, *tell* me," she clamoured excitedly, "what is it, what *is* it?" And seeing that they did not quite understand Mr Hawkins was about to speak again, when Patrick burst out (he so wanted to be the first with the good news!): "Pardon me, Sir, I speak their langwidge," and he turned to Shapian. "Him," he said, giving Mr Hawkins several good hearty slaps on the back, so that he, caught unawares, almost went forward on his face, and his glasses went flying, "That good feller. Him" – here he gave the astonished Mr Hawkins a sound thump on the chest that nearly bowled him over backwards – "him, that's big chief, good, OK. Me – 'tis a difficult tongue, Sir – you, catchem two beaver, chop chop. Savvy?" And finishing in his very best Indian: "Kaygett! Kay*gett!*" he turned triumphantly to Mr Hawkins. "Langwidges was always a gift with the O'Reillys, Sir."

"Quite," said Mr Hawkins. "Most decidedly – ah – yes!" And he smiled as he let the happy party out through the door, and closed it behind them. What an entremely pleasant little game it had been, he thought even if he was after all the loser. And he rubbed his hands together very cheerfully, quite as though he had made rather a profitable bargain.

As soon as Sajo saw the gate of the park, she started to run. She was not pale now, and her eyes, that had been so

121

dry and staring, were all aglow. Her shawl fell back and her braids flew out and bobbed up and down on her shoulders, as her moccasined feet pattered on the pavement. Behind her came Shapian, unable to keep up with her because he was carrying the basket, inside which Chilawee, tired of being cooped up for so long, was making a great uproar. Next came the stalwart Patrick O'Reilly, very red in the face, his helmet off, dabbing with his large red handkerchief at the head that had been "bald as an egg for twenty years".

Once he bellowed, "Hey! What is this, a race?" But the youngsters kept going right on, and it is very doubtful if they ever heard him; so he fell to grumbling, "They'll be the death of me yet, so they will." But he kept valiantly on.

Several passers-by stopped to look at the young Indians in their forest clothes, racing along the street with the policeman apparently chasing them. They heard, too, the shrill cries and wails coming out of the basket, as Chilawee objected loudly to the shaking up he was getting in all this hurry; so a few of them turned and joined this strange parade, and followed this small, running, black-haired girl.

And behind them all – far, far behind – there came another person: a tall, brown-skinned man who strode along so softly, yet so swiftly through the city streets. He looked so hard and stern that people were glad to step aside and let him pass, and stared after him – but he never so much as glanced at any one of them.

There was some delay at the entrance, as the park was not yet open for the day, but O'Reilly soon caught up, and showed his card, and they were let in. Quite a respectable crowd had gathered, and pushed in with them as soon as the gates were opened. The attendant, who was none other than Alec the keeper, already knew what to do, as Mr Hawkins had telephoned him. He had decided, at the last moment, to come too, and now stood in the crowd.

Swiftly, Alec led Sajo over towards the beaver pen. And all at once she was pale as a ghost again. She seemed to be running in a great empty space at the end of which, miles away, was a dark, ugly-looking row of iron bars, and now, now – she could see through them, and there – yes, there was a brown, furry little animal sitting up in the centre of them, and – oh, was it — could it be – yes, it was – Chikanee!

And Sajo, no longer shy, forgot the watching people, forgot the noisy city, forgot everything but the small furry body that was now so close, and rushing to the iron fence she threw herself on her knees in the gravel, thrust her two arms through the bars, and screamed "Chikanee! CHIKANEE! CHIKANEE!

The little beaver, not believing, sat without a move, looking.

"It's me, Sajo. Oh, Chikanee!" The cry was almost a wail. Oh, had he forgotten?

For a moment longer the little creature stood there, stock still, his chubby brown head cocked to one side, listening, as Sajo cried out again: "*Chik-a-nee-e-e-e*!" – and then he knew. And with a funny little noise in his throat, he scrambled, as fast as his short legs would carry him, to the bars.

At that a little cheer broke out among the crowd, and there was a small commotion. And Alec now came forward and opened a small iron gate, and said, "This way, Miss – a – Mam'selle – a – Senorita –" for he didn't quite know how he should address her, and was rather excited himself. And she rushed in, and kneeling down gathered the so-long-lost Chikanee up on her lap and bent over him; and they both were very still. And her head-shawl hid everything; and neither you nor anyone else will ever know just what passed between those two on that fateful, that glorious, that never-to-be-forgotten morning.

And the grey-haired Mr Hawkins took his

handkerchief from his pocket and blew his nose rather loudly; and Alec had suddenly become troubled with ," he cough. "Humphsaid, "hurrumph."

"You bet," exclaimed Patrick in a hearty voice, although the keeper hadn't really said anything at all.

And now was to come the biggest thrill of all. Chilawee and Chikanee were to have *their* party now. They were only a metre apart, and didn't know it! What a thrill was there!

So it was with wildly beating heart that Sajo and Shapian carried the basket in (one of them alone could never have handled this affair; it took the two of them to pull off the lid, they were in such a state); and they lifted Chilawee out, and set him down facing Chikanee, a short distance away. Then they stood and watched, breathlessly. For a second or two neither of the kittens moved, just stared at each other. Then, the truth slowly dawning, they crept towards one another, eyes almost starting out of their heads, ears wide open, listening, sniffing, creeping slowly forward until the creep became a walk, and the walk became a little shuffling trot, and now, sure at last that they had found each other, the trot broke suddenly into a gallop, and with a rush they met, head-on. And so violent was the collision, in a mild way of speaking, that, not being able to go any further ahead, they went straight up on end, and with loud shrill cries they grasped each other tightly, and there, in front of all those people, began to wrestle!

The ceaseless, hopeless searching, the daily disappointments, all the misery and longing, the dreary empty nights of loneliness were over.

Big Small and Little Small were together again.

Before long they were disporting themselves all over the enclosure, and what had been a grim and ugly prison had now become a playground. The crowd clapped their hands, and shouted, and laughed and hallooed at them excitedly, while the wrestlers, or dancers, or whatever you have a mind to call them, stepped around in high feather, enjoying to the utmost what must have been to them the greatest moment in all their lives, up to that time and perhaps for ever after. Never before had they given quite such a brilliant performance; and the people cheered them on, and laughed, and Mr Hawkins waved his handkerchief quite furiously in the air, and I am not at all sure that he didn't shout a little himself.

Patrick O'Reilly, just about dying to take a part in this happy occasion which he had helped so much to bring about, and very proud to think that he was the only one present who knew the whole story, appointed himself Master of Ceremonies, and while he performed his duties as a policeman and kept back the crowd, he also explained to them what it was all about, and cracked jokes, and beamed on everybody in the most amiable fashion, enjoying himself immensely. Indeed, he was entitled to any credit he got, even if he did pretend to know a little more about it than he really did. And when the two Smalls started their queer-looking dance, he was not to be outdone, and was heard to say that it was the very first time in all his days that he had ever seen anything but an Irishman able to dance a good Irish jig!

And then, having been there, watching, for quite some time – for he had not wished to interrupt this little celebration – there now came out from behind the people another figure – a tall dark man in moccasins. He was the same man who, a short time before, had been seen striding so swiftly through the city streets in this direction. A quietness fell upon the wondering crowd as he stepped forward. But Sajo and Shapian, never noticed him until a voice, *the* voice, the one they knew so very well, said softly there behind them, in the quiet, musical language of the Ojibways: "O-ay, the clouds have indeed gone from off the face of the sun. Now my sorrow has gone too, melted away like the mists of early morning. These people have done much – very much – for us, my children. Let us now thank them. My son, my daughter, take up your Nitchie-keewense, your Little Brothers. O-pee-pee-soway is waiting."

Big Feather had come to take them, all four of them, back to The Place of Talking Waters, to the Land of the North-West Wind.

And Sajo's dream had, after all, come true.

CHAPTER FIFTEEN

MINO-TA-KIYAH!

So they said goodbye to the city, with its noise and its bustle and its people, who, after all, thought Sajo, seemed to be just about the same as any other folks – more good ones than bad ones. In fact, nearly all good ones, she decided, and made up her mind to tell the Indians just what they really *were* like.

And they said goodbye to Alec, who had been so kind to poor lonely Chikanee, and who felt very relieved to see his little prisoner free once more; and to the whimsical, quietly smiling Mr Hawkins, who was happy for a long time after, in the knowledge that he had brought gladness to some very sorrowful hearts. And although Gitchie Meegwon had tried to pay him for Chikanee, he would not even hear of it, and said that it was worth the pleasure it had given him.

Patrick O'Reilly brought them to the station and saw them off; and as the train pulled out from the platform, the two children waved and waved to this friend who had been so good, and loyal, and true to them, and he stood there holding his helmet high in the air like a signal, leaving Shapian still firmly convinced that there was a whole nation of people living on a green island in a great salt lake, who called themselves Beavers.

When they arrived at Rabbit Portage, the first person they saw was Yellow Hair, who jumped aboard the boat before it was well landed, to welcome them. Right away, Shapian gave him the money that was left and Yellow Hair told the Big Knives, who were all there to meet them, and offered it back to them. But one of them stepped out and made a little speech, and said that they were very glad that things had turned out so well, and that the Missionary was to keep the money and give it to someone among the Indians who might be poor, and needed it. And Gitchie Meegwon thanked them all for their kindness to his children, and said he hoped that some day it would come *his* turn to help someone, as your turn always came around some time, to do a good deed.

Yellow Hair told them that he was to accompany them back to the village, where he was going to work among the people. And at this the trader, who up till now had kept rather in the background, came forward and said that he was coming too, so that he could become better acquainted with his Indian customers; though he never mentioned, never *would* mention, never *did* mention, that he too had helped. And it never would have been known if Yellow Hair had not seem him that time in the school-house, and told Big Feather about it privately. Meanwhile the two Smalls came in for a great deal of petting and attention, and they even consented to stage a wrestling bout for the assembled Gitchie Mokoman, though I doubt very much if they cared whether anybody saw them or not; and they were rather relieved when the party set out and they were left in their basket to themselves.

Big Feather paddled in his own canoe, which still showed the effects of the fire, and Shapian took the bow. Sajo, on this trip, did no work, but was a passenger, along with Chilawee and Chikanee, who never worked anyway, and she sat with her face stuck into the beaver box most of the time. Yellow Hair and the trader went with some more Indians in another and much larger canoe, one of those great birch-bark canoes called Rabishaws, with a high, proudly curving bow and stern, which gave it rather the appearance of some gallant charger, or a Spanish galleon.

At the first portage they found the old Chief, Stands First, encamped, awaiting them. He asked for an account of all that had happened, and listened very attentively as they told him, and at all the important points and especially interesting places, he said "Hoh!" and "Hah!" and "Hum!" in a deep, throaty voice, and there was a very knowing twinkle in his eye as he listened. And after considering the matter for a while, he told Sajo and Shapian that they were an honour to their people, and that there would be a song made about them, and about their adventures with the Little Talking Brothers, as he called the Smalls, and that it would become a part of the history of the tribe. And he looked in on Chilawee and Chikanee, and said that they too now belonged to the tribe, and would become a great tradition in the nation. And then, pulling his blanket about his waist, he stood there very straight, with his long white hair about his shoulders, and made a sign with his hand towards the sun and said: "Hah! Mino-ta-kiyah; kae*get* kee mino-ta-kiyah! – it is well, indeed, it is very well!"

And all the watching group of Indians, and Gitchie Meegwon, and Yellow Hair, repeated together like a chorus "Minto-ta-kiyah!" and everybody seemed to be very solemn and impressed.

And as they journeyed on their way, on to O-pee-pee-soway, the trees beside the river seemed to wave to one another and to nod, and in the rustling of their branches and their leaves they seemed to sigh, "Kaeget mino-ta-kiyah, it is well"; the ravens in the air croaked, "Mino-ta-kiyah!" and the wind whispered through the grasses, "Se-e-e-e-ey mino-ta-kiyah"; and the racing water in the rapids, that once had seemed to be so fierce and wild, sang it over and over in that strange way that running water has; and the little swirling eddies that slipped from off the paddles murmured it at every stroke, "Mino-ta-kiyah" – to Sajo!

Never had the forest seemed more beautiful, never had the sky been quite so blue; and the sun had never shone so brightly, nor the squirrels frisked as gaily, nor the birds sung half so sweetly, as they did for Sajo, on that journey back to O-pee-pee-soway.

And never had she nor Shapian, in all their lives, been ever quite so happy.

When they arrived, Big Feather called all the people together, and at his cabin that night they held a dance of celebration. Everybody from the village came, including two or three half-breeds who were passing through (and who had *not* bothered anybody's hunting-ground, after all), and who as usual, had their fiddles with them. And there were swift, clever step-dances while the fiddlers played old-time jigs and reels, the players putting into the tunes all kinds of queer twists and turns, after the fashion of the half-breeds; and there were Indian dances with as many as twenty people on the floor at once. And the fun was fast and furious.

All the boys of the village wanted to dance with Sajo, and Shapian was proud to see his sister so much in demand. You may be sure that he had no trouble in finding dancing partners either and there were some very fine-looking young women to choose from, as could be plainly seen, because there was no ducking and hiding behind head-shawls, for none but the oldest ladies would ever think of wearing one at an affair of this kind.

Outside, a huge fire was kept burning, where tea was constantly being made, and before which had gathered a little group of old men who sat and smoked, and talked of the old days, while a crowd of children played tag, and hide-and-seek among the flickering shadows. And Gitchie Meegwon passed among his guests, and talked with them, and his face, that was sometimes stern and often sad, was now very happy and smiling. Every once in a while he went around with a large pail of tea, while Sajo and Shapian carried cups and served the people, and danced in between times.

The climax of the evening came when the dancers

cleared the floor, and sat back in a big circle against the wall, as though expecting something to take place. Soon two drummers took their position inside the circle with tom-toms, and commenced to beat. And then, through the door, came old Ne-Ganik-Abo, Stands First, the Chief, with a great bonnet of eagle feathers on his head and strange, wild-looking designs of paint upon his face, and danced to the sound of the drums. Below each of his knees there hung a circlet of hollow deer's hoofs, that clinked and clanked at every step, and in his hand he held a rattle made of a whole turtle-shell, painted red and black, and having the head and neck of the turtle for a handle. And as he danced, the hollow deer-hoofs fairly rang, like little copper bells, keeping time with the swift movements of his feet, and the fringes on his buckskins quivered and shook, and the great bonnet nodded, and opened wide across his shoulders, and closed and spread again, all in perfect time with the drums, which never stopped beating, and he shook his rattle very fiercely as he danced. And while he danced, he sang a low weird chant, in which he told the adventures of Sajo and Shapian, and Chilawee and Chikanee, the same as in the old days when the warriors had sung the story of a battle. And after each verse there was a chorus, given by a group of singers; and the song had a queer haunting melody that was somehow very exciting.

This was the song he had promised, and it would now be one of the legends of the tribe; for it was by means of such songs about various happenings, and by crudely painted pictures of events, that the old-time Indians kept a record of the history of their people. But the trader, who had never seen such goings on before, and thought it was a war-dance, became the least bit alarmed, until Gitchie Meegwon explained to him that it was not a war-dance at all, but a Wabeno, used only by the Medicine-men, or for the reciting of great events. Then with one loud, long yell the Wabeno came to an end.

And now the fiddles struck up a lively tune, and the floor filled up, and the fun continued where it had left off, and away went the reels and the jigs again. And Yellow Hair danced on nimble feet, and laughed the whole night through, and picked the plainest old woman he could find for a partner; and when things slackened down for any length of time, he got them going again in very short order. And the trader quite forgot his dignity, and footed it as merrily as the best of them. He even made friends with the Smalls, but still could never remember their names, though Shapian, who didn't hate him any more, did his best to tell him.

Chilawee and Chikanee themselves were by no means left out of things; they never would be left out of anything so long as they had two voices to shout with, and four legs apiece to run around on! Excited by the music and the noise and all the fun, they tore about the floor, and scrambled between the dancers, and went around begging wherever they could find anyone sitting down. Once Chilawee took the centre of the room and stood there upright, fair and square in the people's way, and the dance had to be stopped in that particular set, because nobody wanted to trample on the little fellow, or fall over him. For a minute or two he had it all to himself, until Sajo finally had to carry the young ruffian bodily off the floor, kicking and squealing. Meanwhile Chikanee (the saint!), who had lived in the city and knew a thing or two, had found out where there was a case of apples that someone had brought up from the trading post and, discovering that one apple was about all he could cram into himself, he started carrying them away one by one and hiding them, and when he was found and arrested there was a real circus and another squealing match. Hoping to quieten them down, Sajo began giving them chunks of bannock to go to bed with. But they would not stay there,

132

and came bobbing out for more, so they were continually running back and forth with these bribes; and it is very certain that even if they stuffed themselves all night, they could not possibly have eaten the half of it.

At last, tired out with the long journey, and the excitement, and this and that, and one thing and another, they finally retired beneath the bunk; and with their noses tight together, their little hands clutched in each other's fur, and entirely surrounded by bannock, they drifted off to sleep, all their troubles, all the long, weary days of loneliness, gone for ever and forgotten.

From then on, all day and every day, the lake shore rang with shouting and with laughter, as it had done before Chikanee had ever gone away. It began to seem as if such a thing had never really happened, but had been nothing but an ugly dream. The cabin, that for so many days had stood empty and forlorn, was once more filled with joy. And the soft ground at the landing bore again the print of little feet whose owners, those with two feet as well as those with four, had come so near to leaving no more footprints – ever – anywhere.

Chilawee, the rascal, became once again the bold, bad pirate, and was as wilful as he had ever been, or even a little worse. He disappeared as regularly as ever, and could be depended on to be just as regularly found, always up to some mischief or another, and when caught at it would do his absurd, wigglesome dance and fall on his back with a great outcry, either from delight at his prank, or just out of sheer naughtiness. Although they were both beginning to be quite a size by now, Chikanee had given up the race to see who could grow the fastest, and allowed Chilawee to get a little ahead of him. And there he stayed, so that Chikanee was still the Littlest Small, and was as soft and gentle in his ways as he had ever been.

Not that he was good *all* the time; that would have been too much to expect. But many and many was the time

133

when he lay in Sajo's arms, as in the old days, with his nose pushed tight as could be against her throat in just one certain spot that he knew of. And there he would snuggle up, and close his eyes, and puff and blow a little, and make small whimpers of happiness, just as he had done so often in his dreams in the keeper's kitchen. And now he was never to be lonely any more – and he would open one eye and take a look, to make quite sure that he was still there and that it was not just another of those dreams!

And now everything was the same as ever, and the days were very full, and busy, and exciting, with all the swimming and the burrowing, the puddling in the mud and the combing and scrubbing of coats, and the game of hide-and-seek under the canoe, and the wrestling and the amateur building operations on the tiny, crazy beaver house that just never *could* keep out the rain. And then, after all the work and the play were over for the day, the short weary legs plodded up the water-trail to the cabin; and there were the little dishes (the same little dishes!) full of boiled rice, or milk, or, on special occasions, even a little dash of preserves, and then a good stout chunk of bannock apiece to go to bed with, and then the long sleep on a soft, warm bed . . .

And so the happy summer passed.

Came the autumn, and with it the Days of Falling Leaves, the Silent Days. The time had come to take Chilawee and Chikanee back to their old home. For they must now be allowed to take up again the life that was rightly theirs, and follow the Way of all the Beaver People. In the winter it would be impossible to supply them with enough water for their needs, nor could they be moved from place to place, as in the summer. And Gitchie Meegwon called his children to him one day, and explained it all to them very carefully, and told them how the beaver, who would soon begin to grow up, could not much longer remain happy living in such an unnatural was, and that very soon they must be returned to their own folk, to live as the Great Spirit of the Wilderness had intended they should.

Sajo and Shapian had known for some time that this must be so, though they had never mentioned it to one another. As the day for the parting drew near, Sajo became very quiet and thoughtful, and spent long hours with her Little Brothers, who would soon be hers no longer; while they, as happy as a pair of sand-boys, played with her in the same old ways, with never a thought for the days to come, even though they should be happy ones.

And she loved them so much that she would not think of how lonely *she* might be after they were gone, but of how glad *they* would be to see their father and their mother once again. So how can I be sad, she asked herself, and then said aloud, in rather a quavery little voice, "I'm very happy. I *am*. I *know* I am!"

Yes, Sajo, you were happy; happy as must be, always, those who give.

And so, one morning in October, in the Month of Falling Leaves, when the hills were all crimson, and brown, and golden in their autumn colours, Chikanee and Chilawee, Little Small and Big Small, took their leave of their little private room and the cabin where they had spent the happy, carefree days of kittenhood. And they left the shaky little beaver lodge, and the water-trail, and all their landing-places, left them there behind them on the shore, and climbed into their old birch-bark basket that had served them so well and for so long, and embarked on the last and most important journey they had ever made.

And little did they guess, as they settled themselves down on their scented sweet-grass beds, how great an event was waiting for them at the other end of it.

135

CHAPTER SIXTEEN

IN THE MOON OF FALLING LEAVES

It was to be a big affair.

Sajo wore her many-coloured tartan plaid, her newest, brightest head-shawl and her beautifully beaded moccasins. Shapian and Gitchie Meegwon had on their best deerskin clothes, worn only on very special occasions, and newly smoked to a rich, velvety brown. On the famous basket Sajo had painted leaves, and many-coloured flowers, and birds and little animals, to be company for Chilawee and Chikanee on this the last of all the journeys they would ever take in it; and with a big white feather hanging from the handle, and all the painted pictures, it looked no longer old, but like a new one. In it, with loving care, she had arranged a bed of sweet-scented grasses, and had tied to it, in a little leather bag decorated with porcupine quills, the two small, but very precious dishes.

The canoe, that had served them so staunchly and so well, and had shared so many of their adventures, had not been overlooked. No signs of the fire were left upon it. Its sides had been dyed a bright yellow, as before, and it had newly painted gunwales and a new eye (not so fierce as the one it had lost – rather a jolly-looking eye, come to look at it), and also a fine new tail. And a very proud appearance it made, as though it knew very well that this was to be no ordinary voyage; and out in the wind it wagged its new tail in a very frisky way indeed, and the eye, as the reeds and rushes blinked and nodded past it, seemed to be winking to itself as though its owner was very pleased about something or another.

And so they headed for the River of Yellow Birches, that lay far away in the blue distance among the Hills of

136

the Whispering Leaves, where Chikanee and Chilawee had been born.

For six days they journeyed on. And ever, as they went, the air grew more still, the waters calmer. Every night long strings and lines of wild-geese flew overhead towards the south, the beat of their wings sounding very plainly in the darkness. Each morning the sun seemed a little larger and redder, the leaves more brilliant in their colouring. For the forest, in the days of Indian Summer, in the Moon of Falling Leaves, is very beautiful.

Sajo was really, truly happy; not at all as she had expected to feel. To keep herself that way, she kept remembering that her small, so-well-beloved friends, her Little Brothers, were going to be better off than they had ever been, and that they were going home, home among their own folks. Their play-days were almost over, she knew; they were becoming more sober-minded. Soon they would be going to work, as all the forest animals and nearly every kind of people, must do sooner or later; that, she agreed (did you ever notice how easy it is to agree with yourself?), was what they were made for, not just to be pets, but to work; which was quite true. It was the only way that they could ever be really contented.

Yet there would come, once in a while, a little ache in her heart, and she would say to herself, "I'm just sorry for *me*. That's only being selfish. We must do what is best for *them*. That's how much I love them." And she would look bravely around at the trees and the lake, and peep into the basket, and tickle the funny, pursey ears, and think how lovely it would be if only she could just see what went on, and hear what they said to each other when they got inside the lodge.

If only their father and mother and the other little ones would come to meet them, so she could see them all together! And she hoped – oh, how she hoped! – that no hunter would ever find them.

On the last night of the journey, they camped among the ere so long ago, Gitchie Meegwon made his noon meal beside the little stream that came down from the beaver pond. And on this memorable night, after supper had been eaten and everything put away, and it was dark and the camp fire was blazing away cheerfully, Big Feather said that he had something of importance to tell them, something that he had been keeping for the very last.

And everything was very quiet beside the glowing fire. Even Chilawee, who sat beside his basket, not moving at all, his head cocked to one side, beaver fashion, seemed to be listening; and Chikanee, lying with his head on Sajo's knee, quiet as a mouse, must have been listening too. The broad, deep river, that flowed so silently and swiftly by, must certainly have heard it all, and no doubt repeated it over and over to the very first rapids that it came to. Even the great, dark trees that stood so solemnly and still around the camp, seemed to stand and listen also.

"Sajo, Shapian," said Gitchie Meegwon, "this is the last night we will spend with Chikanee and Chilawee. Tomorrow they will be back with their own people, to live in their own way. Very pleasant have been the days they spent with us. They have brought much joy to our house, and the bright days of summer have been brighter because they came to us.

"I found them at this place, sick and helpless – dying. Now they are back here again, well and strong, ready to carry on. Their adventures are over, and they will be happy as never before. One thing I can promise: they will never be killed."

Here Sajo made a little sound, a very little sound, but she put her finger to her lips to push it back in. Gitchie Meegwon went on:

"You saw your Chief dance the She-she-gwun, the Dance of Rattles; it was a Wabeno, for a special sign, and

138

he has commanded that no Indian shall hunt beaver in or near this place. And here no white man ever comes. This is my own hunting-ground, but I myself will never harm them, or their family; it would be like killing small, friendly people. For they have made my children happy; could they understand me, I would thank them. Come what may, they will be forever safe.

"Tomorrow, when you let them go, I will give the call of a beaver, the sound with which they call to one another. The young ones in the lodge will not listen, but perhaps the old ones may come and greet them. I cannot be sure, but I will try."

Just then a low moaning cry came floating out from somewhere in the hills, became louder for a while, and faded again to silence; a wild, deep-toned wail – the cry of a wolf. Gitchie Meegwon paused until the last echo had died away, while everyone listened; for Indians do not fear the wolves as some do, but look on them as fellow hunters, calling them The Lonely Ones.

Then he continued: "Big Small and Little Small," – he smiled at the names – "will never be quite lost to you. Beaver are different from other animals; they are very like persons, and do not quickly change. Once they know you and have become your friends, they do not forget. They will be yours, always.

"And now the best thing of all. Once every year, in the Moon of Falling Leaves, when the leaves of the forest are falling all about us like brightly painted, red and yellow snowflakes, and the wild-geese fly in clouds across the sky, then you shall come here, to their home, and stay a little time and watch beside their home-pond, and see them swimming, working, playing. It is very likely that they may come to you, so you may speak to them, perhaps may even touch them. They may not be able to remember everything, and many of the things they saw with you may pass from their minds, but *you* they will *never* forget. The old men, who are very wise, have told me. In my young days I, too, have seen it.

"My children, those are my words."

And they were words that took out from Sajo's heart the last traces of sadness – not *quite,* perhaps; for after all she was giving up everything she had to give – these two tiny creatures that she loved so dearly. But they were not forgetful little people, her father had said, and, she thought, I will hang the basket on a tree, near the ground, and leave the little dishes too, where they can come and see them, so they *won't* forget. And that night, as she lay on her bed of balsam boughs, with Big Small and Little Small sleeping cuddled in her arms for the very last time, she thought over everything that had ever happened, since they had come to her on that never-to-be-forgotten birthday. And she thought of everything that her father had said – he was going to call them, and maybe the old ones would come out, and everything – and it seemed a shame to sleep away this very last night of all. So she lay awake as long as she possibly could, listening to the quiet breathing of Chilawee and Chikanee, until at last she passed with them into the land of dreams.

The next afternoon, just as the sun was setting, at the time when wild beavers awake from sleep, they were all beside the home-pond of the Beaver People, from which Chikanee and Chilawee had started out on their Great Adventure that had now come to an end.

In most ways the place was much as it had been in May, the Month of Flowers. The dam was full and running over, and in the best of shape, and the house still reared itself like a huge, dark mound, high above the fen-land. But the pond no longer looked to be deserted. Fresh work showed everywhere, making it appear more than ever as though a gang of men had been busy with axe and shovel. Yet all this was the work of two beavers, for the little ones

140

do not count for much during their first summer. The sides of the lodge had been all heavily plastered to keep out the cold, and floating out in front of it was an immense raft of logs, and sticks, and branches, which had been collected for the winter food supply. From different places along the shore, smooth, well-kept, narrow roads wound their way up into the woods, and alongside them a number of freshly cut stumps were visible, the very teeth-marks plainly to be seen upon them. Most of the trees that had belonged to them had disappeared, and were now hidden away under the raft, and a few others lay near the water partly cut into lengths, showing where the Beaver People were still at work, gathering in their harvest.

It was very quiet and peaceful there, and the ring of silent trees was reflected very clearly on the calm surface of the water; but their tops were no longer green, but were red, and yellow, and brown, where the frost had painted them. And all around through the silent forest, the falling leaves came drifting, spinning, rustling slowly down.

Gitchie Meegwon drew away a short distance, while Sajo and Shapian carried the basket down to the water's edge between them. And there, beneath a tall, silvery poplar tree, they opened it.

Shapian reached in the stroked the plump, silky little bodies, and said, "Farewell, Nitchie-kee-wense; good-bye, Little Brothers"; but not very loud, because his voice was a little shaky, and a man had to be careful about such things. And then he took his sister's two hands in his own, and said to her: "Do not sorrow, my sister. Every year when the leaves, like now, are falling, I will bring you here. Many things have we four seen and done together; we will always remember, and *they* will not forget. Our father has said it. Now they will be happy, all their lives. It is well with them."

"Yes," she answered in a whisper, "I know; they will be happy. So I must be happy too." And she smiled up at

141

him, "Thank you, my brother."

Then Shapian went over and stood with his father, and left Sajo there alone. She held the little beavers close, just for a moment, and whispered into the small black ears: "Goodbye, Chilawee; goodbye, Chikanee, my Little Brothers. Don't let's forget . . . *ever*."

And then she let them go.

She followed them to the very edge of the water, where she stood watching them as they floated off. On they swam, on across their own home-pond, their two round chubby heads side by side, as they had always been; sturdy Chilawee, jovial, wayward and full of whims; gentle Chikanee, wistful, winsome and affectionate. A few more minutes and they would be gone. And no matter how big they might grow to be, in one tender, loving little heart they would still remain two tiny, helpless baby beavers.

To Sajo they would for ever be the Smalls.

As they drew near to that great stronghold across the pond, Big Feather gave a long, clear call, the call of a beaver looking for his companions. Again the sound, like a note of music, stole out into the stillness; and again. And then, quite suddenly, a black head appeared on the surface of the water near the house, then another; great dark heads, with big furry brown bodies that floated high behind them.

Sajo scarcely breathed; just what she had hoped for, but had not dared to believe – their father and their mother were really coming, at Gitchie Meegwon's call, to meet them! Everything was coming true, *everything*–.

Everyone stood as still as the trees themselves, while the old beavers came slowly towards Chikanee and Chilawee, passed around them once or twice, looking, sniffing at them, making some low, thrilling sounds, and then swam on beside them – big heads and little heads, all together now! Swimming steadily and swiftly on (oh, all too swiftly!), they held on to their course, the water streaming out wide behind them in long, rippling V's; and once or twice there could be heard the faint, distant sound of child-like voices. And the dark heads, the big ones still close beside the little ones, became smaller and smaller, farther and farther away, until, right before the entrance to the lodge, one by one, without a sound, they sank beneath the surface, out of sight.

Big Small and Little Small were Home.

Sajo stood there very still, like a many-coloured little statue, in her tartan dress and pretty moccasins, her head-shawl fallen back and her glossy black hair shining in the glow of the setting sun. And so she remained, looking out over the little pond, with her red lips parted and her dark eyes bright and starry, watching until the last brown head was gone, and the very last ripple on the water had disappeared.

And just then, from among the golden, whispering leaves above her head, there came the rippling notes of a small, white-throated singing-bird. His voice seemed to fill the quiet valley, and, to the ears of Sajo, he sang a message, of hope, of happiness, and love: "Mino-ta-kiyah, it is well," he seemed to sing. "*Me*-me-me-e-e--*no*-no-o-o--*no*-ta-kiy-*no*-ta-kiy--*no*-ta-kiy--ah!"

And Sajo, standing there so quietly among the falling leaves, her eyes still fixed eagerly on the dark mound that was the last home of her Beaver People, repeated softly to herself, "Mee-no-ta-kiy-ah."

And the little basket, with its two tiny dishes, its bed of scented grasses, and its painted animals and leaves and flowers, she hung upon a low branch near the ground, and left it there beside the clear, still water.

Then turning, with outstretched hands, and bravely smiling, she ran to meet her father and her brother.

IS THE STORY TRUE?

Yes, Grey Owl, who wrote it fifty years ago, said that it is. It was told to him by Sajo and Shapian, who would have been nearly fifty themselves, for it took place about the year 1905. At that time the Indians in the remoter parts of Canada were living much as they had done before the white man arrived. The area where the story is set was later included in a National Park – parks which were set up so that the wilderness should remain unspoiled.

Like Gitchie Meegwon, Grey Owl rescued orphaned beaver kittens and brought them up in his cabin. His close contact with these playful, trusting little animals changed his life. Before he had the kittens he had made his living by trapping animals, then selling the skins for the fur trade, now he decided to hunt no more. Instead he wrote articles about the great forests and lakes, the birds and animals – especially the beaver – which he knew so well. His writing was noticed, his work to save the over-hunted beaver was given government support, and he was made a warden of one of the National Parks. He spent the rest of his life in a log cabin, on a lakeside, miles from any other settlement of people.

Who was Grey Owl? He was born in England and as a child he had been fascinated by the North American Indians. He learned all he could about them, and when he went to Canada as a young man he lived with Indians and was accepted into the Ojibway Tribe – Sajo's tribe. Through his writing he brought the life of the Canadian wilderness to a world-wide audience. He took up the cause of all wild creatures and, because of his crusade, beaver-hunting was made illegal in most parts of Canada.